PADMAVATI, THE HARLOT
and other Stories

These are stories of a rare and adult feminism, capable of seeing man as son, lover and god. It is a disposition associated with the majestic women of the epics. In Kamala Das this universalist tradition has astonishingly survived. But is the man of the present times capable of mirroring these visions of totality dreamed by woman?

In answering this question Kamala Das does not make woman an outsider. Her woman abides by man. She lends her mind and consciousness to function as absorbents for man's presumptuous, sanctioned one-sidedness. Spirituality and a search for god become incumbent for such a woman. And the most obvious figure Kamala Das can utilise to serve as an embodiment of this condition, which is not one of dumb resignation, but one that is driven to fill a moral vacuum, is that of the prostitute.

Kamala Das's stories are a re-affirmation of woman, woman reclaimed of body and spirit. But it is woman, above all, always on the side of life, never betraying it by antagonising man through mean acts of getting even, or scoring points.

What they say about the bestseller 'My Story'
by
Kamala Das

It is a straightforward story... it has sincerity that strikes an immediate rapport with the reader.
—*Sunday Standard*

...there are entire sections that are marvellously written.
—*The Hindu*

Among the best things I've read... is the turbulent, self-indulgent but at all times frank story of Kamala Das.
—*Deccan Herald*

The present reviewer, a woman, enjoyed reading the book thoroughly.
—*Business Standard*

Kamala Das does not hide her secrets and does not follow the rules of old morality.
—*Assam Tribune*

The chapter headings accentuate the "Excitement" ....There is enough in it to give... readers the "sizzle" and "spice"....
—*The Times of India*

...the verses from the writer's own repertoire... speak highly of her poetic talent.
—*The Tribune*

The technique and structure of the book are remarkable... the life portrait of the cosmopolitans is quite pictorial...
—*National Herald*

My Story describes a life of frolicking in sex.... The book has its accent on titillation.... The titles of chapters are revealing.
—*World Literature Today*

Published by
Sterling Publishers Private Limited

PADMAVATI, THE HARLOT
and other Stories

Kamala Das

A Sterling Paperback

STERLING PAPERBACKS
An imprint of
Sterling Publishers (P) Ltd.
L-10, Green Park Extension, New Delhi-110016

Padmavati, the Harlot and other Stories
©1992, Kamala Das
ISBN 81 207 1389 3
Reprint, 1994

All rights are reserved. No part of this publication may be reproduced, stored in a retrieval system or transmitted, in any form or by any means, mechanical, photocopying, recording or otherwise, without prior written permission of the publisher.

Published by Sterling Publishers Pvt. Ltd.,
L-10, Green Park Extn., New Delhi-110016.
Printed at Ram Printograph (India), Delhi-110051.
Cover Printed at Crescent Printing Press, New Delhi
Cover design by Biplab

CONTENTS

1. Moongphali 7
2. That Woman 14
3. The Princess of Avanti 16
4. The Sea Lounge 19
5. Padmavati, the Harlot 23
6. Equity Shares 26
7. The Youngman with the Pitted Face ... 33
8. December 36
9. A Little Kitten 38
10. Darjeeling 40
11. The Sign of the Lion 41
12. Sanatan Choudhuri's Wife 45
13. The Coroner 49
14. Iqbal 53
15. The Tattered Blanket 57
16. Leukaemia 61
17. A Doll for the Child Prostitute 65
18. Walls 102
19. Grandfather 107
    Glossary 110

1
MOONGPHALI

When Jasmit Ahluwalia had just finished washing her four-year-old daughter Bittu, the autorickshaw stopped near her house. It was her mother, on her usual annual visit from Gurdaspur. You normally come only two days before Guru Nanak Jayanti, Mother, Jasmit cried out in surprise, of course I am happy that you are here sooner than expected.

I had a bad dream two days ago, said the mother, alighting with her painted trunk. I dreamt that our darling Bittu was crying out for me.

Bittu, releasing herself from Jasmit's clutches, rushed forward and hugged the old woman's knees.

I shall not give you one paisa more than what I had promised you at the railway station, the mother told the rickshaw driver. I am an old widow, living alone in Gurdaspur, selling milk to make both ends meet. I shall give you five rupees and nothing more.

But I have not asked you for more, good mother, said the driver, casting admiring glances at Jasmit's golden legs, displayed below the folding of the salwars. If you do not want me to take any money from you, continued the man, say so, Mother, and I shall go away without a word of protest.

The old woman pulled out from her bosom a cloth wallet, and took out a five-rupee note. The purse was swollen, Jasmit noted with pleasure.

After the autorickshaw pulled away from the *mohalla*, Jasmit asked her mother if she would care to have some tea. The old woman was immediately upset. How many times have I told you that tea is not good for the skin? No wonder you look so old, although you have not crossed thirty. You have lost your fresh pink complexion. Don't you take *lassi*? Rohini is giving me eighteen pints of milk a day, can you believe it? I keep a pint or two and sell the rest. I have brought you a tin of ghee, hard as a brick and three hundred rupees to open a post office account in our Bittu's name. You are very generous, Mother, said Jasmit, watching the child climb into the old woman's capacious lap.

And, how is your intellectual husband, the Masterji, the old woman asked. Does he still return late at night?

You know well how good he is to me, Mother. He does not go out to meet bad women, or to drink at bars. He goes to give tuitions in order to make enough money to feed me and the child. From each tuition he makes sixty rupees. In fact he gets more money from the six tuitions than from the school he teaches eight hours a day.

Times are bad, daughter, it is not right that you are left alone in the evenings.

But this is not an unsafe place, Mother. Everybody knows us. There is nobody in this *mohalla* who will want to harm me.

There are other communities living here too, said the old woman. There are Hindus too....

But what is wrong with the Hindus, Mother? They are as good or as bad as the Sikhs.

So you have started to abuse the Sikhs, cried the mother, rolling her eyes. She held the child tightly against her bosom as though to still the palpitations of her heart. Jasmit, you do not know what has been happening to our community in the recent months? Does he not read the papers, your brilliant Masterji? You know what took place at the Akhal Takht. How can such an act be ever forgiven?

I don't know these things, Mother, said the young woman, I am not a woman who bothers about politics. I look after my child and feed my husband. These are my only duties. Let the Prime Minister look after the country.

Wah! wah! wah!, what a brilliant little speech! You are indifferent and lazy, that's what you are. You don't care if your community gets humiliated, do you?

Moongphali, moongphali, shouted the vendor from outside the door. I have some *shingada* too for our darling Bittu....

Who is that, asked that old woman frowning, hurriedly depositing her grandchild on the floor. The vendor was a man of about seventy, carrying a basket on his head. He put it down on the stoep of the house and said, peering into the dark interior, *Behnji*, give me a drink of warm water if the *sigri* is already lit. This is a cold morning and my chest is acting up. One can hear the whirring inside. It is like a machine turning, an oil press..

How dare you ask my daughter to get you hot water? Who are you to take such liberties in this house?

The vendor folded his hands and smiled at the old woman. I am well known in this *mohalla*, big Mother, but this is the first time you are meeting me, perhaps. I am Gurcharan from Dacca, but I have been living in Delhi since the partition. My only daughter Sita went away with her Muslim lover. Nothing could stop her. She became a Muslim and married him. I do not hear from her. She has forgotten her father, because I thrashed her with a stick when she told me of her lover. Now whenever I see young women of her age I remember her and cry. Don't I cry often, Jasmit *Behnji*?

Yes, you do, said Jasmit. Where are the *shingadas*?

In silence the old woman watched the man take out from a roll of red flannel the gleaming water-chestnuts. He removed his *sigri* from the basket and placed it on the ground. He blew into it, turning the coals red hot. The smell of groundnuts, roasting spread in the air. Bittu's nostrils dilated. *Chachaji*, give me some moongphali she cried, thrusting out a pink palm. The vendor held it to his face and kissed each finger tenderly. Yes, yes, golden princess, you may have your moongphali, he said, grinning.

He had lost a front tooth, and the remaining ones were reddened with betel. Oh, he is certainly a devil, thought the old woman, feeling uncomfortable, watching Jasmit lounge in her wet and crumpled clothes, exhibiting without shame the rounded calves of her legs and the contours of her comely bust. Buy the groundnut and let him go, said the old woman gruffly. Let the good man carry his wares to the others in the colony.

Big Mother, I am not in any particular hurry, said the vendor, I am not even in need of money. I have enough at home in a tin to feed me for a whole year. I come out to sell groundnuts only to meet people. I am lonely at home. There is no laughter in my *jhopmdi*. Outside I hear the children's laughter. I hear the soft talk of women. Such sounds make me feel good inside.

I was not blaming you for anything, said the old woman, subdued all of a sudden by the sincerity of his words. I was only warning my daughter not to trust strangers. Times have changed, especially for us Sikhs. For no fault of our own we are being harrassed.

Here we are safe, Mother, said Jasmit. Everybody is friendly towards us. Why, Bittu's father's best friends are all Hindus- Shuklaji and Devidayal. They are like his blood-brothers. When he falls ill they visit him twice a day and bring him medicines from the vaid at Pusa Road, the *Madrasi* doctor.

Arrey, the Masterji is back, shouted the vendor, why is he running towards us?

Jasmit watched her husband running along the road towards their home. What is the matter, she asked, her voice suddenly shrill. Has the school-house caught fire?

Her husband seated himself down on the *charpoy* in the yard and removed his blue turban. He was perspiring although the winter breezes brought only an icy chill. Is anything wrong with you, Son- in- law, asked the old woman. You look as if you have seen a *bhooth*.

No, Mother, not a *bhooth*. I saw human beings who were more frightening than any *bhooth*. They were killing people like us. She has been killed.

Who has been killed, asked the old woman.

Give me some more moongphali, *Chachaji*, cried Bittu. Indira Gandhi, said the young man.

It is God's will, said the old woman. What else did she expect, sending her army into the Akhal Takht?

Shut up, Mother, said Jasmit. You do not know what you are talking about.

She was shot by her security guards, both Sikhs. And now the Sikhs are being killed. Massacred all over the city. I ran all the way home. I was afraid they would have reached here. Who are killing the Sikhs, the old woman asked, Pritam, tell me who are killing the Sikhs? The Hindus?

I do not know, Mother.

Why should you assume that they are Hindus, asked the vendor handing some nuts to the child.

What are we to do, asked Jasmit. If they come here what are we to do?

What can we do against so many, asked her husband.

What kind of an attitude is that, Son-in-law, shouted the old woman. If the Hindus come and molest your pretty wife you will not lift a finger to save her, is that your attitude? You are a rotten coward. You are not a man. You are a disgrace to the Sikh community.

Mother, stop calling him names, said Jasmit. I told you last year that I cannot stand your abusing Bittu's father.

All right, Daughter, I shall not complain. After all, I am only an old widow whom nobody loves. I came bringing you ghee and three hundred rupees to start....

Run into the house, cried the vendor. The mob is here.

He pushed Jasmit into the house and set the child in his basket covering her with a red cloth.

Wear a saree and come out through the back door, *Behnji*, he told Jasmit.

Where will you take her, Gurcharanji, asked the husband. I shall take your wife and child to my *mohalla*. I shall tell everyone that my daughter has returned from Pakistan. Cut your hair and run for your life....

And what will happen to me, cried the old woman, beating her bosom wildly.

The mob was nearing their house. They had already set fire to the six houses at the beginning of the road, the houses where their friends were living. The flames glowed pale in the winter sunshine. Blood for blood, the mob shouted.

Go and fight, you eunuch, cried the old woman, pushing her son-in-law out of the yard. Don't behave like a coward. You are a sardar and never for a moment should you forget it....

She went inside the house and locked the door. The vendor had departed, carrying Jasmit and the child with him. The old woman cursed him in silence.

Footsteps approached the yard. Brothers, what have I done to you, asked the young Sikh, his voice trembling with unease.

The old woman heard her son-in-law groan twice. Then she heard the mob abuse him. Set the house on fire, someone shouted, but she felt that she was rooted to the floor. Fear had paralysed her. She wanted to pray aloud but no sound rose from her mouth.

At Lajpat Nagar, the vendor's neighbours said, Pakistan must be a good place to live in. Judging from what you have been telling us your daughter must be at least fifty-four. But she looks hardly thirty. Good food, they must be eating, the Pakistanis...

Sita, these are all my good neighbours, said the vendor. Make some tea for all of them and give some milk to the child. Yes, Pithaji, said Jasmit, in perfect obedience.

2

THAT WOMAN

We heard of father's death from the local barber. Three years ago, father had left us to live with a young woman. And yet when mother heard the news, she swooned. When mother regained consciousness, we set off for the street where father had lived. I wanted to snatch from the woman any will or testament she might have got my father to sign.

When I reached the house, I found the woman seated on the floor, her face buried in father's bosom. She was weeping softly.

"Have you forced father to make a new will in your favour?" I asked her.

She raised her reddened eyes to mine. She did not speak. I did not feel any pity for her. "Legally, you have no right to his property," I said. She did not speak.

"Are you planning to harass us?" I asked her.

"I shall not harass anyone," she said.

"In that case, please get up and leave immediately," I said. "In half an hour's time, our relatives will reach here. It will be unseemly for you to be seen here."

"Where can I go?" she asked faintly. I felt that she was asking the question not to me, but to father's corpse. Her eyes were full.

"You may take all your things. You do not have to leave your belongings here," I said, suddenly softening in my attitude towards her.

She kissed my father's feet twice. Then she walked towards the door and paused as though she had forgotten something.

"No... there is nothing of mine remaining here," she said.

As she walked along the street in her crumpled cotton sari, I expected her to look back at least once but she did not. 'Ah, Sthree'.

3
THE PRINCESS OF AVANTI

The old woman who believed herself to be the princess of Avanti had come to the park as usual with the packed lunch provided by her daughter-in-law. She hid the packet carefully behind a bush. Then, stretching out her spindly legs, dry and blotched by mosquito-bites, she began to curl a strand of hair, twisting and coiling it round her finger.

Three young men in shabby clothes walked up to her and greeted her with folded hands.

"Namaskaram, O Princess of Avanti," said the tallest. "We do hope that you are in perfect health."

His companions laughed. The old woman joined in the laughter good-naturedly.

"My health is perfect," she said, "but I am not able to curl my hair today. If I cannot curl my hair, I shall not be able to wear my crown."

"That is a grave problem," said one of the men.

"Today is your wedding day. Naturally you must wear your crown," said another.

"Is it true?" asked the old woman. "Is it at last my wedding-day?"

"The whole world knows that today is your weddingday," said the tall man. Otherwise, we would not have travelled to this city.

"Have I met you before?" the old woman asked.

"No, we are new here," said the man. This young man is the King of Vangarajya. The other is the King of Kerala. I am the ruler of Kalinga. We want you to select one of us as your husband."

The hag smiled happily. She had lost two of her front teeth. When she smiled, her tongue showed through the gap.

"I am certainly glad to meet the three of you," she said. Then as if to show that she was shy she closed her eyes. The empty smile remained on her face.

"We have come to ask of you a favour," said the King of Vangarajya. "This evening you must not go home. Remain hidden behind a bush. After the park is locked we shall climb over the wall and come to you. We can celebrate your wedding quietly inside this beautiful park."

The old woman clapped her hands. She threw her hair forward and then from behind its grey strands she peeped out at the young men. "All right then. We shall see you tonight, O Princess of Avanti," the King of Kerala said, bowing to her.

"We love you passionately," said one of them.

"Do not disappoint us," said another.

"No, I shall not disappoint you," said the hag.

At night, they were with her once again.

"Suppose she cries?" asked the tall one.

"I can prevent that," said the second.

"She desires you," said the third.

"What do you want from me?" asked the woman. She had a quavering voice.

The young men removed her dress. She had no undergarments. One took a long look at the sagging breasts and guffawed.

"Don't hurt me," cried the woman.

"O beautiful one, we are your husbands," the King of Kalinga told her, nibbling her ear-lobe.

"Oh, you hurt me terribly," the woman cried out. "I cannot bear this pain. Do not bite me to death."

She struggled to free herself from their grip.

"Keep quiet," said one of them. "If you utter one more word, we shall kill you."

"I am not the real princess of Avanti," the old woman said between loud sobs. "I do not like to get married."

"Keep quiet, you old bitch," said one of them, panting like a train taking off from the platform. Another young man closed her mouth and nostrils with his rude red palm.

"Is she dead?" asked the tall man. The woman's legs had stopped thrashing in the air.

"Is she dead?" he asked his companions.

"Perhaps," said the youngest.

Translated from Malayalam by the Author

4
THE SEA LOUNGE

Before climbing the stairs, carpeted in maroon and white, to wend his way towards the Sea lounge, Satyavrata had already rehearsed his lines about a dozen times, but reaching the plate glass of the door he paused for a moment, feeling a sudden sense of panic. Would she weep, would she once more proclaim her passionate love for him as she did in her last two letters and create now an unsavoury scene? Did he choose the wrong place for the meeting? The Taj was nearly always full of people who knew him well. Perhaps at the Sea Lounge he could manoeuvre her to sit behind a potted palm or at the last table in the row of tables looking out at the Apollo Pier. It was not easy, of course. She was fond of making herself conspicuous by wearing quaint clothes. Don't I look a real nut? she had asked him one day last year when he ran across her at the shopping centre. She had worn a red scarf tied round her throat and had a pair of jeans with four ridiculous patches stiched on. What if she came dressed like that to the Sea Lounge? Oh he would die of shame.

As soon as he pushed open the door to enter he saw her. She was sitting at the second table gazing forlornly at the sea. He followed her gaze and saw the evening sky, the sea, still blue and vivid and the white sails of the boats, bulging with the wind. He sat down opposite her and said Hello. She turned her face very slowly and smiled at him. I am sorry I am a few minutes late, I got held up at the office, he said. She nodded. I have already ordered for myself, she said. A gimlet. He signalled to the waiter and asked for a hamburger and coke. Don't you drink ever? she asked him. I am not too well today, he said fumbling with the menu card, feeling nervous.

I must be totally sober he told himself. I must not allow liquor to change my mind about the girl. He had to tell her frankly that he did not wish to marry her. He was grateful for the love she gave him, the kindnesses in her letters and in her conversations with him whenever she came to the city for a holiday. But that was all. He was going to be ruthless with her. It would not do to let her dream on about a future with him. She was not his kind of woman. A real nut, she had called herself. He liked his women sophisticated and feminine. I do not want to beat about the bush, he said, looking her straight in the eye. I do not want to marry you. In fact, I do not wish to marry for another ten years.

The glass of gimlet in her hands began to turn slowly. A goblet of thin crystall with its pale liquid and a slice of lemon floating over it. She noticed for the first time that her fingers were long and extraordinarily lovely. She wore on the middle finger of her right hand a ring, set with blue stones, which matched the cerulean blue of her silk saree. She had brought into the hotel along with her blue saree and the ring, the essence of the sea. She had become an extension of the sky, the blue sea and the sailboats. Why had he missed noticing her pure grace, he wondered, feeling uneasy. But the die was cast. She said, that is all right, I understand, please don't have a guilty conscience about me....

Your father had rung me up yesterday, he said. He felt clumsy while he bit the end of his hamburger.

Yes, he told me, she said in her cool voice, but do not worry about Papa, I shall explain the position to him.

But he wants you to get married before he leaves for the United States next month, he said, hoping that she would once again talk of her need for him, hoping that she would give him another chance....

I will marry my old beau, she said, the one who has been crazy about me for years. Let us not worry about it now. Tell me about your new job.

While he talked about his superior, his landlord and all his friends, she twirled the stem of her glass, looking into it intently as though it were a crystal in which she could see her future and his. He was entranced by that gesture. The whiteness of her hands danced before his eyes. Outside, the sky was turning dark. Were her eyes darkening too? he wondered looking with astonishment into their serenity. He left half the hamburger in his plate and wiped his mouth. This is no good, he said, I don't think I can finish it. She miled. It is time for me to leave, she said, and very soon they were out of the Sea Lounge walking together down the steps, she admiring the floral design on the carpet and then stopping for a minute at the bookstall to open the first two pages of a glossy magazine and moving away to walk out of the hotel. May I get you that magazine, he asked her eagerly but she said, halting on the marble steps, oh no they are all so expensive, thank you all the same. Her hair began to fly, wrapping half of her face for a second and settling back again. She was beautiful. With an ache in the pit of his stomach he realised that all the beauty of his life was going away with her. She was going away from him with no promise of a letter or a meeting. Everything between them was ended. In panic he said, may I give you a lift, I can drop you wherever you want to go....

She shook her head. No, I want a walk, she said, laughter floating up in her voice, it is a lovely evening going waste, I want a long walk, thank you all the same.

She turned to the left and walked on past the new annexe called the Intercontinental and then on and on among the evening revellers, past the little wooden stands where men sold dolls made of shells, and disappeared from his view. Then the dusk set in.

5
PADMAVATI, THE HARLOT

When Padmavati, the middle-aged harlot, finally reached the foot of the shrine, climbing the seven hills and stumbling along the winding passes that separated each from the other, dusk was a giant bird with its wings spread out, shading the temple, the banyan tree and the stone lamps in which the oiled wicks burnt on feebly. She could only see the outlines of the shrine, when she paused to peer upwards. I am late, she said to herself, hitching up her saree and proceeding to go up the steps. The loafers loitering around approached her and looked at her plump calves with lewd smiles. Shall we help you, lady, they asked her, noticing the red blouse that she wore, the tinsel in her hair and the betel stain on her full lips. I have come from the city to see the Lord, she told them. I have been wanting to come here for the past thirty-three years but something or the other has kept me busy all this time. At first I had to tend my ailing mother who lay paralysed for seven years before she died one day, turning her face away from me in disgust. Then I had the responsibility of educating my brothers who got good jobs in other cities and forgot me. I had also to marry off my sister to a man who was willing to do it for a big dowry. After the marriage, she has not once written to me. But I am not complaining. Who can blame them? Who will want to consort with a woman like me? Only idlers like you bother to talk to me. Nobody loves me. Only the Lord, perhaps, has any feeling for me. But He may have forgotten too.

You talk too much, lady, said one of the young men. You are not young, but you are charming enough for one evening or two. Your breasts are still firm. Your haunches set our loins on fire. Wont you be kind enough to grant us your favours?

The rest of the group laughed aloud. The woman was flushed with anger. Do not make such requests to me at this moment, she said. I have come to see the Lord. This is not the right time for such talk.

What is in your hand, asked a young man pulling at the basket she was clutching. It is a basket of fruits, she said, I am taking it up as an offering. The young men removed it from her hand and began to eat the fruits, spitting the pips out noisily. Your Lord cannot eat these fruits, but we can, they said laughing raucously. She felt her eyes moisten with tears. You are brutes, she said, you have no pity for a woman old enough to be your mother....

You are not our mother, said the young man who had spoken to her first. What is your name, lady?

My name is Padmavati, said the woman.

Padmavati, you have arrived too late, said the young man. The shrine is closed for the night and the *pujari* has left for his home. You cannot see your Lord.

But I cannot return to the city without seeing Him, said the woman. I have been walking from morning to be able to reach here for the evening's puja. What can I do now? Keep us company this night, O Padmavati, said the idlers. Tomorrow you can worship the Lord.

Padmavati turned and walked up the stone steps to reach the temple yard. The door was shut. The lamps were burning low. She looked around in fear. She could not see the young men at the foot of the hill. Even the leaves of the banyan did not move. In sudden terror, she rushed to the heavy door and knocked on it with her fists. Then the door opened, its hinges whining. She lowered her eyes. She saw only the feet with their bejewelled toes, but she fell over them with tears flowing from her eyes. She kissed the toes with love. Help me, O Lord, I am only a poor harlot, she cried. I have always wanted to see You but until today I did not get a chance. I was busy looking after my family, lending my body to strangers who hated me and then hated themselves.

Padmavati, rise, said the Lord, embracing her with His arms. She could hardly see His face. It was dark inside the sanctum sanctorium. I have nothing to give You, she said. I had brought some fruits in a basket but the loafers at the foot of the seventh hill snatched it from me. Now there is nothing to give. If You were a man I would have given You my body, stale and ageing, but You are a God. What can I give You?

She felt the warmth of His body against her own. She closed her eyes in ecstasy. At dawn, she left the precincts of the shrine and walked down the steps with her hair dishevelled and her blouse torn in places. She blushed like a bride when the young men at the foot of the hill came near her and looked at her face. There were bruises on her cheeks and on her white throat. Her lips were swollen and blue. There was fatigue in her eyes. She hid her face behind her long hair and walked fast. The young men let her pass, bowing before her and murmuring, Mother, go in safety, give us your blessings and go your way....

6
EQUITY SHARES

When the middle-aged lady arrived in her maroon Ambassador, Velayudhan was helping his eighty-year-old mother feed the cows. He was so surprised to see a visitor that he nearly dropped the pail, half-filled with gruel, enriched with OK cattlefeed.

His mother ignored the guest for a minute or two. Then she nodded towards the car and said, "I did get your letter, but I wanted to give you my answer personally, that is why I did not write to you..."

The visitor smiled. Velayudhan enjoyed the warmth of her smile. He had not seen such a friendly smile for years. His mother had stopped smiling after the death of his younger brother 23 years ago. When they brought the crushed bits home tied up in a bundle his mother screamed as though she had been seized by the devil.

"Please don't open the bundle," she had cried. "I don't want to see his remains...."

The visitor followed his mother into the large sitting room. Velayudhan opened the windows to let the air in. The place was dusty. The shapeless cushions had split here and there and the silk cotton was in the air. He sneezed once.

"Please sit down," said his mother. "We live here, Velayudhan and I. The maid servant has left early today. I apologize for the disorder in the room. We seldom open this room, now that we are alone in the world. When Velayudhan's father was alive, he used to receive his visitors here every evening. Visitors came even from far off places like Travancore and Cochin."

Velayudhan kilted up his dhoti. All of a sudden he felt ashamed of his not- so- clean clothes. The lady, however, did not seem to be noticing them. She looked at the stacks of books and the old dinner set in the cupboard.

"They are my children's books," his mother said, following her gaze. "Venu's and this Velayudhan's. You would not believe it, but this son of mine was normal once. He was first in his class in the second standard. Of course, that was before he fell ill. In those days, there was no medicine for typhoid. The delirium lasted too long. That was how he became what he is now. Everybody used to admire his smartness. And his looks. He was fat and fair. His hair was curly, just like his father's. And now, see what has happened to his looks. Thin and dark, like a piece of firewood."

Velayudhan laughed at the comparison, envying his mother's smart way of talking. If only he could talk like her, he would get visitors too, and maybe, friends...

"I do not see anything abnormal about your son," said the lady looking at him. Her eyes were lined with kohl. There was a red dot on her forehead which fascinated Velayudhan. It was a perfect circle. She could not have applied the dye with her fingertips. He had seen their maid servant dress her forehead with sindoor, applied with a spatulate fingertip. She used to wash her face before returning home every evening. And she would thrust a flower or two into her hair while passing through the garden. But that was a long time ago. Before the bad phase. Before the fall from the staircase that made her a lifeless doll with a bleeding head.

When the police came, he was sent into the dark attic to hide.

"Do not open your mouth," his mother had said, giving him some bananas to eat. "Remain there till they go away. Otherwise they will take you to jail and beat you with their lathis...."

That was a long time ago. He had almost forgotten the girl's pretty face. And the way she used to let him caress her breasts when they were behind the cattle-shed.

"You know well why I have come," said the lady. "If you are interested in selling the shares, sell them to me. My family owns nearly half of the existing equity shares. If we get a hundred more, we get to control the company. You have no such ambition. I could give you a neat lakh or two which you can put in the bank..."

"We don't need the money," said Velayudhan's mother. "We have enough money in the bank for our needs."

Velayudhan's bosom swelled with pride. His mother was behaving like a thoroughbred. She was determined to hide their abject poverty. Even an offer of two lakhs was being spurned. He laughed, covering his mouth. The visitor went pale. She wrung her hands in an unfamiliar gesture. Velayudhan laughed again.

"I know how sentimental you are about the shares," said the lady. "After all you got them from your husband who gave his life to the company, working night and day. But you preserve the papers just as you preserve all his possessions, his reading glasses, his sandals, his medicine bottles."

Velayudhan's mother nodded. The visitor had seen the mementos, the sandals, the reading glasses, the medicine bottles...

"Velayudha," cried the old lady, "please bring a tender coconut for our guest. This summer is the hottest I have ever known. You must be dying of thirst."

"Please don't trouble yourself," said the visitor. "I have had my tea already."

"We do not take tea," said Velayudhan's mother. "We drink only buttermilk. If you want some buttermilk, my son will get you a tumbler."

Velayudhan rose from his seat with alacrity. He was beginning to like the visitor. He liked the way she glanced at him secretly from the corner of her large eyes. Perhaps she was getting attracted to him. Like the maid-servant who had allowed him to touch her breasts. Yes, this one had lovely breasts too, like water-melons tucked into her silk blouse. Perhaps one day she would...

"Velayudha, don't stand staring at our visitor," cried his old mother. "Bring her a tender coconut and a few plantains."

Velayudhan forced himself to leave the room. He was getting irritated with his mother. Was the old woman growing jealous of their pretty visitor? She did not want him to make a good impression on the lady. He sliced off the top of a tender coconut and emptied it into a glass. Then he took a small sip. He felt a delicious churning within his abdomen when he thought of the lady's lips, touching the spot that held the imprint of his lips. When she drinks from the glass, she would, in some inexplicably mystic way, become his bride.

When he neared the door he heard the lady say, "With the money he could open a grocery shop right here in your compound. There is no such store anywhere near this place. He would then feel better, with something to do. A man needs to feel that he is the breadwinner...."

"He does not need a shop. He has plenty of money in the bank," said the old mother. "Why should he work when he is so rich?"

"You may be right," agreed the visitor. She did not look happy sitting there with her chin cupped in her frail fingers. Velayudhan wanted to rush towards her and take her in his arms. After all they were meant to meet. Meant to love. Otherwise fate would not have sent her to his house in the afternoon when even the trees were enjoying their siesta. The flowers on the hedges were asleep too. The cows were sleepy with food and comfort. If only she had arrived a few minutes later, when his mother was asleep in her room she would have been his visitor, not his mother's.

"This is good," said the visitor, sipping the drink, her eyes smiled above the rim, met his, in an embrace. Velayudhan blushed. He sat down on the floor and hugged his knees.

"Velayudhan, don't sit on the cold floor," cried his mother. "You will get your arthritic pains again."

"You must keep quiet, Amma," he said. "You must not order me around the whole day as though I am only a child. I am forty-eight this year. Have you forgotten my age, Amma?"

"You are acting very foolish today," said the old woman, rising from her seat, "You must leave this room at once. Go upstairs to your room and lie down. This lady wants to discuss something very important with me. We do not want you to hear our talk."

"I shall remain here," said Velayudhan." I am not a child."

"Let him remain," said the visitor. "After all, there is nothing secret about my offer. He has every right to hear. After your time is over he is the one who will inherit the shares. He might decide to sell them to me."

Velayudhan's mother shook her head. "No, that is not likely to happen," she said. "Velayudhan will not sell his father's shares. In fact he will not sell anything that once belonged to his father. I get offers for this house, my estate, my rice-fields, but I refuse to sell. Why should we sell when we are rich?"

"If we are rich, where is the money?" asked Velayudhan. "I do not get any money from you except for a haircut once a month. What are you doing with the money?"

He knew that he was annoying his mother. But he was all of a sudden so ashamed of his mother's habit of telling lies that he wanted to expose her to the visitor. What was the use of bragging of wealth when the sofa was torn, the cushions torn, the dhoti torn....?

"Velayudha, go this minute upstairs to your room," cried his mother, pushing him away. "The police van is on its way. I can hear its rumble."

Velayudhan scrambled out of the room and panted up the stairs. Inside the little room he felt safe. Blood thumped in his ears. He shut his eyes with work-worn hands. "No, I did not kill her," he shouted. "She slipped on the banana peel and fell down the stairs. I did not kill her. I only watched her fall..."

From within the sitting room the visitor heard his shouts and felt uneasy. "I must go," she said. "If you are not thinking of selling the shares why should I waste your time?"

"You must try to understand," said the old woman. "They were bought by my dear husband. I cannot ever sell any of his belongings. He wanted Velayudhan to become a director of the company. Or Venu. Venu was crushed by the school-bus. So he cannot ever become a director of the company... and Velayudhan... he is not well now. Perhaps when he gets better he could become a director. I hope you will try to understand..."

"I understand," said the visitor, softly. From his room upstairs Velayudhan shouted out once more, "I did not kill her!"

When the visitor got into her maroon car, the old lady said, "Of course, your offer was not a bad one. Two lakhs is a lot of money. But when my son gets well he will want the shares to become a director."

The visitor nodded, starting the car. "Yes, he will become a director," she said. "Why not?"

7
THE YOUNG MAN WITH THE PITTED FACE

It was only a month old, the relationship between the dying woman and the beautiful young man. He was the youngest, the loveliest man she had ever loved, and the situation frightened her.

She had during the past fortnight two major operations and the cardiac condition which had worried her doctor, had remained. Her womb, that had lain fallow, had grown fibroids just as a desert may grow cacti and carnivorous plants. Her liver had adhesions. Her intestines, not to be outdone, had developed Tuberculosis. All this and the weak heart had in those recent months drained her of whatever beauty she had left. The Chloroquine that was administered regularly made her colour as dark as quinine. And yet, being a woman, nothing but a woman, she rubbed lipstick on her blue lips and washed her hair everyday to leave it sweet-smelling.

The young man used to visit her at the hospital room long after the evening visitors had gone. There was a No Visitors board on the door but that ignored the kind ones, because everyone seeing her knew that only kindness could save her.

Going on the trolley with the abdomen shaved and the skin all anointed with Acriflavin and the lint wrappings covering her like an Egyptian mummy, she was not even sure if she wanted to be saved. If she survived she would return to the narrow confines of her brown body and the little flat with the blue brocade curtains and her favourite bronzes but if she slipped out of the surgeon's hands silently, beautifully she would be free, she would have the universe with its celestial furnishings as her home.

She would be in the wind, in the sea, in the rain, in the sand on the beach where the young man walked with his wife. And at night, the young man would tell his wife the winds are cold and sharp today, close the window, and without knowing that she was at the window the wife would shut it and lie against his body.

She was given two pills to help her at night, a sleeping pill and a painkiller to muffle the aches. The third blessing meted out to her was the beautiful young man. He held her hand in his and sat still until she became sleepy. Then in a hurry, with a shrug of his nervous shoulders, he would leave the room. When she asked him if he could love her, her eyes full and her mouth pale he would look down at his shoes and say, you know what you mean to me.

Then, she was brought home. Everybody was tender to her. She longed to see the young man. He promised to visit her in the morning, and this thought kept her brave during the night when she told her husband that she did not want her sleeping pills and painkillers that night. Pain was like the murderer returning to the scene of crime.

At night, the surgeon's phantom-scalpel scoured the vacant spaces inside her. She said tomorrow he will be here with his pitted face, his over-plump thighs, his beautiful teeth and tomorrow he will again take my hand in his and everything will be beautiful for those few minutes.

But although she waited after her nurse had washed her and powdered her like a baby, he did not come. In the afternoon he rang up to say that he was busy. The next morning he would come. She lay awake with her pain, ignoring tranquillizers.

In the morning, her nurse dressed her up like a bride, knowing how deeply in love she was. But the young man did not come. Who is going to tell her the reason for his not wanting to continue with that strange relationship?

8
DECEMBER

She had just recovered from a long illness and was looking thin, and her skin had a muddy hue but he looked at her through his sunglasses and said you look all right, are you all right now? She nodded and hurriedly took his hands between hers thinking how perfect his hands were with the fingers smooth-skinned and sturdy, the nails square and the palms soft like a woman's, and, she asked what shall we do today, shall we just sit here and talk? It is cold outside, and, he said, I thought you were to come with me to my place today, don't you want to see my room? Yes, she said, yes, of course I must see your room and left with him going down the curving staircase pressing his left arm to her side.

In the car, he turned once to look at her and asked her, what are you thinking about, and she smiled not saying anything, for how could she tell him that she had, when very ill, promised God never to sin again, repeating several times, Oh God, I shall give him up and think only of you. The promise had worked but she was going to break her word and with no great qualms either. I was worried about you, he said, you don't know how I worried about you, and she touched his knee and smiled.

It was a windy morning and when she got out of the car and walked with him past the lawns and on the gravelled path leading to the cottage, she shivered slightly, and, he said, are you sure you are warm enough, you ought to have worn something thicker, but she shook her head murmuring no, no, I am not feeling cold...

The walls were rough and painted a dull terracotta. As usual, there were books all over his bed, new and fresh-smelling and she picked them up reading their titles and smelling the jackets and laid them on the end table near the alarm timpepiece and the green ashtray. Lying down, stretching her legs, she thought happiness is so simple, just walk into his room and lie down and I am happy, but I am a happiness-addict, that is my problem....

He removed his coat and sat down near her, looking down at her face and into her eyes with his red bleary eyes and she stroked his face running her fingertips along the wrinkles and over the blemishes, knowing deep inside that only when alone with him could her frustrations vanish, and then, even the fact that she had not written one good line of poetry for the past several months did not seem to matter at all. I am no good at anything these days, she thought, and I know now is how to make love to this particular man. What makes you smile, he asked her suddenly, laying his head on her breasts and she kissed the top of his head murmuring, my sweet, my sweet, not answering his question, and for a long time afterwards they were both silent in that room with only the alarm timepiece ticking away and a bee humming from somewhere behind the window.

Are you happy, he asked her and she nodded, while tears rose in her eyes and not seeing those eyes, he asked, you don't have any doubts, do you and, she kissed his eyes shut with feverish lips, whispering no, no, not anymore, but though I have become soft and sentimental, I shall never be able to write again, I am finished....

9
A LITTLE KITTEN

When they had finally settled themselves down after weeks of honeymooning in a small flat at Dadar, she told her husband that she felt miserable and lonely from eight in the morning to six in the evening while he worked in his insurance firm at the heart of the city. If only you could get me a pet, she murmured, nestling closer to his chest, a little kitten, even a kitten would be such a comfort...And, he threw back his head and laughed. What a sweet and innocent creature he had married! He tickled her until she rolled over on their double bed and screamed out for mercy. You are killing me, please stop, PLEASE STOP. Then, he began to lick her toes, numbling, you see, I am your kitten, I am your little kitten.

After three months of ardour, they began to quarrel. Nothing very serious, of course. Just a few probing queries regarding his relationship with Miss Nadkar, his secretary, and his mysterious silences that would last for hours. Speak to me, I cannot bear these silences. Leave me alone, he would say and disappear into the bathroom.

One day, she climbed upon a stool and peeped into the bathroom through the ventilator. He was seated on the edge of the tub, frowning. What are you doing there, she shouted at him. He got up and pulled the ventilator shut. It nearly snapped off her fingers. No wonder she was angry and frustrated.

When they were on the best of terms she used to take a bath in the evening after tea and buy a jasmine strand from the flowerboy to hang from her long plait. She had naturally pink cheeks but on tiring days when she saw herself pale she cheated a little with a touch of rouge which she kept hidden away. When Miss Nadkar was unwittingly drawn into the orbit of their life together, she stopped taking the evening bath. The flowerboy went away disappointed.

Even the old Maharashtrian woman who used to wash the vessels for her in the morning, began to wonder what had gone wrong. She had lost her bridal freshness. There was a new crease on her brow which sliced the red *bindi* in two halves. Pimples began to form on her cheeks. She found herself worrying about her digestion.

Then, one day he came home dead drunk after attending an office dinner. She tore her wedding saree into shreds. She grew frighteningly hysterical. Would you like to visit your parents for a month, he asked her. You look as if you need a change. She was alarmed. She went to look at her face secretly in the bathroom mirror. He was speaking the truth. She had lost the glow which she had before she settled down at Bombay. They were living close to a mill. She felt that the smoke from its chimney was darkening her skin. Yes, I need a change, she told him. But you will have to come with me....

He gave for the first time a birthday gift to his secretary because he had begun to compare her with his petulant little wife. Miss Nadkar was serene. In fact, he had once heard the clerks teasingly calling her Her Serene Highness. He thought it clever of the clerks. When he gave her an ivory figurine on her birthday, Miss Nadkar blushed very nicely and murmured: You shouldn't have spent so much money on me....He had done it on an impulse. After all, he was not the demonstrative kind. And she was Miss Nadkar to him although once she had asked him to call her by her name, Indira. I heard that you were planning to leave us soon, Miss Nadkar, he said. The office will miss you. She blushed again. The marriage will take place only in December, she said. My fiance will come from Canada in October. Still four months to go. And looking up into his eyes, she flashed a smile, a gleaming jet of a smile that made his stomach quiver.

That was their first evening together. They went to dark, smoke-filled restaurants and took always the cornertable where they could sit half-concealed behind potted cacti. At home, his wife sulked and lost her looks thinking unkind thoughts incessantly. Once or twice, she put all her silks inside a trunk and decided to go back to Dharwar, but he dissuaded her. What will your parents say, he asked her.

One day, when he came back home, warily crossing the hall to go to their bedroom, he found his little wife seated before her dressing table brushing her wavy hair. She turned her face to smile at him. He was taken aback. She looked so pink and healthy. There was a gleam in her dark eyes, a secret message for the male. He rushed forward to embrace her. You look so pretty, he said. So pretty and happy. Then he saw above her breasts a long red scratch. What happened, he asked her. Did you find yourself a kitten? He looked around. Perhaps, it was hiding somewhere in the kitchen. Is it a stray, he asked her. She kept silent. She was looking over his head to a spot in the dusky sky. What are you staring at, he asked her, I don't see anything there but some clouds, some smoke....

10
DARJEELING

When she was picked herself up from the floor where she had collapsed with a sudden heart attack she looked to her neighbours like a fish just taken out of an oven, all steamy with sweat and open-mouthed. Her eyes held intense astonishment but were dry. Her four-year-old son who had sensibly called the neighbours in, kept murmuring in her ear, *Amma, Amma,* are you all right, are you all right, stroking her damp forehead with his warm, crayon-stained fingers. The family doctor was sent for, and before he arrived, the ladies lifted her on to a bed and re-arranged her saree covering her knees properly. A pale crescent of flesh was visible beneath her blouse but they did not dare to touch her chest. It was obvious that her heart had a seizure.

The doctor phoned her husband and in not so cheerless a tone told him that he was shifting his wife to the hospital immediately. He was about to phone for an ambulance. The husband mumbled, thank you, doctor, thank you, I shall be home in ten minutes. I am so grateful. He was at that moment thinking of the red silk saree that he refused to buy her on her birthday, using her middle age as an excuse. We are both no longer young, he had said, even the Prime Minister said that the middle aged must not celebrate their birthdays... Too late, too late, cried his conscience. He rushed into his boss's cabin and finding it empty, scribbled an explanatory note and ran out of the office with his linen-coat slung over a shoulder.

In the ambulance, she lay still and silent and at her feet sat the child who had begun to like the fast ride and the sight of motorists veering to a side making way for them. The husband sat on the narrow seat opposite, clutching the doctor's letter and brooding over his finances. There were hardly two hundred left in the bank. If she were to die today, the twenty-eighth of August, he would not be able to give her anything better than the electric crematorium. The only friend who could be trusted to lend him money was touring the United States of America. If she were to pull herself through, the hospital would fleece him all right. Her diamond earrings could be sold. But who would look after the child?

The ambulance gave a lurch as it turned the corner to enter the wide black street edged with stalls selling smuggled razors and perfumes. She moved her lips slightly. It seemed as if she was trying to pray. The red saree, the red silk saree, shrilled his conscience. It would have enhanced the gold of her skin. If he had given it to her, she would have gone with him to the Shanmukhananda Hall to hear Balamurali sing. Although malnourished and frail she had class. Whenever she wore dark colours and wove flowers into her hair all the men in the Shanmukhananda turned to look at her.....

The ambulance stopped in front of the hospital and two wardboys rushed forward to carry her off on a trolley. They looked so very dark, so very sinister. He thought they were like Yama's servants. He said, wait a minute, let me get her admitted. The wardboys flashed great big smiles. The bed is ready in the ICCU, said one of them, the doctor saheb had phoned, you only have to sign your name at the registration counter, we shall take the mem saheb in. The doctor is waiting in the ICCU.

They took his wife away in the trolley pushing it into the lift while its wheels clattered like weird laughter. His child pulled at his knee. Pick me up, *Appa*, he cried, I am sleepy. He had a tear-stained face. Why are you crying, he asked his son, lifting him up, you were so brave, so well-behaved, what has happened now, your *Amma* is going to be well in two days' time, and then we shall go for a holiday to Lonavala. Or perhaps Darjeeling. She has always wanted to see the snow.

When he entered the Intensive Cardiac Care Unit carrying the sleeping child on his shoulder, she was lying tranquillized in one of its cubicles. The large hall, partitioned into cubicles by white, seemed like an oasis where the weary travellers of the desert had come to pitch their tents for the night's rest. Her heartbeats magnified by the machine beside her bed sounded like drums of doom. Suddenly, he shivered. The honorary called him aside and whispered, it is all right now, she is sleeping. It was a heart attack, there is infarction, but I hope to see her recover in a fortnight's time. It is rare in women of her age, she can't be past thirty-five, what, thirty-nine, I wouldn't have believed it, did she suffer any mental strain, any secret tension?....I don't think so, said the husband, she is not the worrying type, I do all the worrying at home. Ha, ha, laughed the doctor, you can leave the worrying to me now, Mr. Raghavan, now you may go home and get a good night's rest.

At night, after he had fed the child with rice and a laddoo which his wife had made in the morning and had given brave and cheerful answers to all his questions, he sat down to write the letters. He had to inform his father-in-law. Then the older children who were at the school-hostel. Perhaps that could wait, but the letter to the bank had to be written. As my wife has just had a heart attack and has been admitted to the Intensive Cardiac Care Unit, I request you to grant me an overdraft of five hundred rupees. He liked the solemnity of the sentence. At his office, he was used to being envied for his drafts. Why, only last week his boss had called him to his cabin and said, Raghavan, years ago I had the good fortune to work under Mister Eswarayya, ICS. I tell you, Raghavan, nobody in India could write English prose as crisply as he could. I was going through your report submitted to me yesterday. Raghavan, in preparing drafts, you are second only to the late Mister Eswarayya, ICS....

Appa, when are we going to Darjeeling, the child asked, suddenly sitting up on his bed. I thought you were asleep, said the father. He went to the child and lay near him. The child's mouth smelled of ghee. Sleep moved like a wisp of mist blurring his eyes. He embraced his father. We must go to Darjeeling, he said, *Amma* wants to see the snow....

11
THE SIGN OF THE LION

I met him for the first time in December last year. I had of course seen his arrogant face many times in the newspapers. When I met him, he was already out of power, and had lost his popularity. The peoples' dailies condemned his attitudes. One of them published a photograph showing him in the traditional pose of the convict. He was trying to hide his face. Every copy was sold out by evening.

I was stepping out of a shop, and he was entering it. We collided. He looked tried. I saw around him the sad aura of a king in exile. Did the beggar-maid meet a disenchanted Corphetua, an Asoka Priyadarsin, after his Kalinga? Would Alexander have noticed her?

A faded beggar-maid. But later he said, we are in love. I believed him. His dark skin reminded me of Krishna. The libertine. The inconstant lover. The monarch. I kissed his small mouth. Every movement of that mouth charmed me.

When he was a little boy in a village, his mother got the gypsies to tattoo a line between his brows.

She called him Kanhai.

He was born in August, under the sign of the lion, Leo. Grow your hair, my lion, I told him. Let your mane grow, and I will bury my face in its harsh glory...

Some people desire to climb a mountain. Some people wish to go to the moon. All I ever wanted was to possess someone superior.

Is he my superior?

The room where we make love is furnished like a study. But there are large mirrors on three sides and a couch in the dark corner. The mirrors inhibit my love making. I feel that I am taking part in a group orgy. He has a habit of looking into the mirrors now and then. When he does that, I close my eyes. Why do you love me, he asks, holding me close, why do you love me so much? I do not know how to answer that question.

At night, from the invisible jungles, from the lush foxholes, his concubines wail: Oh Krishna, come to me. I clasp him to my breasts. I cuddle him. The women wail no. The night is his damp skin. Its breath is his breath.

He is afraid of the dark. Once, when I switched off the lights, he clung to me. What are you afraid of, my baby-boy, I asked him. Do not be afraid. I am with you.

They say that he is old. They say that he is untrustworthy. I tell them to leave me alone.

I am never secure. That goes without saying. If my feet were secured on the ground, my mind would fall asleep. But this way with my feet off the ground, my mind leaps, it flies.

He is a rich man. I am moderately poor. The rich, I think, are supermen; they are on their way to becoming Gods. Once when we were waiting for the lift, outside his door, a servant told him that the lift was out of order. This annoyed him, and he kicked at the grill. What nonsense he said. The lift came up.

His life is simple. After love making, a little bit of sleep. After sleep, some politics. His taste tends to be crude. His servants fill a Ming with artificial flowers. There are statues of national leaders in his drawing room. He calls John O'Hara a serious writer. There are John 'O Haras in his bookcase, and Sherlock Holmes.

Is he now inside me, or outside with the darkness and the ghosts?

Beside the rivers of my blood, he rests like a hunter after the hunt. The rivers wash away his thirst. He drinks my blood. He grows strong on my meat. With a trim sandalled foot, he kicks at my nerves. They sprawl all over the earth like the roots of trees felled years ago.

His dead face floats on the waters of my dream. It is a blue lotus. He asks me to be faithful to him. My mind writes a requiem for this unsatisfying love affair. He smiles in his sleep.

He is the Brahmin husband who comes in a red palanquin a little before midnight to lie near his Nayar wife. She will be the dark rider on the pale horse of his lust. Before the east pales they part.

Before the cock crows thrice, my beloved shall betray. He shall deny me. Will he one day ask me to stay? Will he one day be able to separate my face from a sea of faces?

I hold him in my arms, I lull him to sleep. His slow fingers learn the contour of my breast.

My friends warn me. You will end up dead. They want to know what happened to the typist he had some years ago, the one who was going to have a baby. They want to know where the film extra has gone, the dark girl who used to visit him in the afternoon.

He clings to my breasts. He is my baby. People say that he will discard me. They say that he will take me to Lonavala and with tenderness kill me.

I tell him of the child to come. He will be a little lion, I tell him. A beautiful lion-cub.

His eyes wander. He is absent-minded today...

12

SANATAN CHOUDHURI'S WIFE

His marriage was six years old when Gopi Menon began to have a suspicion that his wife was deceiving him. One morning, two hours after midnight he woke up and drowsily moved closer to his wife. Still half asleep and without opening her eyes at all she embraced him and whispered: "Sanatan, my love...."

Sanatan. Whose name was it? Menon could get no sleep afterwards. Even when the brilliance of the sun entered through their window he was lying awake and afraid in the snuggery of her arms. But he was too proud to rouse her from her slumber to ask her about the mysterious Sanatan.

When she was making breakfast in the kitchen, he opened her wardrobe to have a look at her clothes. How did she manage to buy for herself all those silk sarees? He had given her one during last Diwali. But there were more than fifty silk sarees in the cupboard, swinging shimmeringly from their hangers. She carried the tray to the bedroom asking, what are you searching for in my cupboard?

How did you get so many expensive sarees, he asked her. Aren't these genuine Kanjvarams?

Kanjvarams? She laughed aloud. The canine tooth that protruded a little made her mouth prettier. He had always thought that her smile resembled Audrey Hepburn's. These are sarees one can pick up for ten rupees. They are art-silks brought here by a man from Matunga who sells them to all the ladies in this building, she said, still laughing in mirth.

When he was standing on the platform waiting for the fast train to Bandra, he suddenly decided to put her to a test, to clear his own mind of suspicions. He returned home immediately.

When he reached the end of their street, he stopped in surprise. His wife was coming out of their house swinging a handbag, and wearing a blue saree. He hid behind a lamp-post. She was walking fast to the taxi stand. He caught a taxi and followed her. At Ridge Road in front of a huge house surrounded by a garden, she stopped her cab. She opened the gate and disappeared into the house. He dismissed his taxi and loitered near the gate. He could see the heavy door of the portico open and a servant greet her with a salute. Then the door closed again.

Menon walked around the house and reached the open window of a large room at the back which he recognised as the dining room. He peered in through the panes. His wife was seated opposite an elderly man at a large dining table, and was busy eating her breakfast. The man was in a silk dressing gown. After she had finished eating, she rose to kiss the man gently on his forehead. He fondled her for a minute. When she left the room, the man lit a cigarette and began to read the newspapers. Menon was shocked. Was she capable of such deception? This girl born and brought up in a Kerala village? How could she enter another man's house, eat a Western-style breakfast with him and allow him to fondle her? Oh God, let this be nothing but a nightmare, prayed Menon.

With a new-found courage, he walked up to the portico and rang the doorbell. Open the door, he roared out to the inmates of the house. A servant opened the door and scrutinised his shabby work-clothes with disdain.

I must see your master immediately, said Menon.

The Saheb and the Mem Saheb are having their breakfast. You will have to wait for a short while, said the servant. What is your name?

My name is Gopi Menon, said the aggrieved husband.

In a few minutes, the host came to the door. He extended his well-manicured hand to Menon. I am Sanatan Choudhuri, he said. What can I do for you?

I heard from somewhere that you wish to let out a portion of this house, said Menon. I have come to find out if it is true...

Somebody has been playing a practical joke on you, said Choudhuri. This was built ten years ago according to a plan drawn by my wife herself. All four of my children were born in this house. So neither my wife nor I will ever dream of letting out any part of this house to strangers.

At that moment, she entered the portico. When she saw Menon, she quickly covered her head with the edge of her saree and tried to return to the interior of the house.

Wait for a second, Mrinalini, said Choudhuri. This poor gentleman was led to believe that we were letting out a portion of our house. Somebody was obviously trying to tease him.

She smiled pleasantly, revealing the prominent canine which made her smile so special, so Audrey Hepburnish. Somebody has been trying to fool you, she said.

I am sorry to have bothered you in the morning, said Menon.

That does not matter, said Choudhuri.

Goodbye, said Menon and walked away without looking back at the couple watching him from the shaded portico. Outside the gate on the grey cemented pillar there was a brass plaque with the name Sanatan Choudhuri chased on it. Menon could not bring himself to give a backward glance at the lady wearing blue although she resembled his wife to a remarkable degree. Suspicion is a kind of poisonweed, he told himself as he walked to the nearest bus stop.

13
THE CORONER

When Sylvester Louis Gomes went to each of the twenty-four flats to collect rent for his aged master who lived all by himself on the ground floor of the sixty-year-old building called the Rose Manor, he normally wore his blue shirt and a pair of khaki shorts that swirled round his thin flanks like a skirt.

But on Wednesday, the fourth of November, he knocked at the tenants' doors dressed in a shiny teeshirt made of black nylon and a pair of dark trousers that obviously belonged once to his stout master. The married lady on the first floor who was expecting her first baby gave him a genial smile. You are three days late, she said, running inside to fetch her purse. Sylvester allowed himself to perch on the cane settee, on its very edge, and saw under it a cat lying fast asleep in a flat basket filled with torn woollen socks. The lady was probably mending her husband's socks, he said to himself. He felt warm and quite at ease in the company of virtuous women. The girls on the top floor who went out with strangers every night made him very uncomfortable. They haunted his thoughts, torturing the serene forest of his mind with loud shrieks like young parakeets. Several times, he had told his master of their nocturnal movements but the old one, shrewd businessman that he was, only chuckled and said, Sylvester Louis, live and let live. And counting the currency, he would say, money is after all money...

Mister Gomes, will you have a cup of tea, asked the young lady, handing him a cheque. No, Miss, only a glass of water if you please, said Sylvester. When he was sipping the iced water, she sat on a chair and said, you don't look well today. Have you been ill?

Not ill, said Sylvester. A tragedy happened in my family this Sunday. Then for the first time, she noticed his black clothes. Oh I am so sorry she said, cupping her narrow face with both hands, I hope it was not someone very close to you....He smiled wanly. It was somebody very close to me, Miss. It was my only son Richie, I have talked about him to you. Richard. The one who got the salesman's job at the Handloom House. His twenty-third birthday was to be in December. He was born on the twenty-fourth. When he was born my uncle Reggie told us that we should call him Noel. So he was christened Richard Noel Septimus. He didn't do so well at school. Got plugged so many times. But just before his S.S.C. exam. his mom promised Our Lady of Mahim a novena and so he got through with a high third. Even the Father at this school, the Principal was surprised. Richie was like that, a good-for-nothing fellow, fooling around with girls before he was sixteen. The Father used to meet me outside the church after the morning mass and he used to say, I am sorry for you Sylvester, you are a god-fearing man but you have a very heavy cross to bear, your boy is a born repeater and if he goes on at this rate he will pass the S.S.C. only by the time he reaches forty...His mom spoilt him. Him being her only child and so fair-skinned. Gave him money, stealing from my pocket at night, and he went to the cinema and smoked, and danced with the bad girls, but I could do nothing. My wife has been having T.B. for so many years, Dr. Pereira is treating her, he gives all the sample-medicines free like the Iron Pills and the Liver Extract but she is still so thin, so weak, and if I beat her she will fall down and die...

But how did this happen, asked the young lady. Her voice was so melodious and sad that the cat stirred itself and opened its eyes. Sylvester smiled again and tugged at the neckline of his teeshirt as though it was choking him. He went with his friends for a swim, Miss, he said. After grub he got up and left carrying his bathing trunks and a towel. Don't swim on a full stomach, his mom told him. He had eaten well. His mom is a good cook. Every Sunday, no matter how tired she is, she prepares for us a good solid lunch. It is either mutton in gravy or pork vindaloo. She says the Good Lord, He wants us to eat well and rest on Sunday.

That day, it was pork. Richie ate in a hurry. Then he called out from the verandah to his pals who were waiting for him on the road. They went to bathe in the sea off the Cuffe Parade, you know where the Tamilians have made little huts of tin. He got cramps. People saw him wave out for help. They thought he was fooling them. He was always a great one for fooling everybody. One day, he came into the kitchen dressed up to look like a girl with lipstick on his face and some rags thrust inside his shirt. Then he holds out his hand at his mom and says, Halloo Missus Gomes, How nice to meet ya...Oh how, his mom laughed! When she laughs too much she coughs. It is as bad as weeping for her. Happiness never killed anybody, she used to say. But it was happiness that killed my boy. He was so happy and so full of fun...

Oh it's terrible, cried the young lady. How will your poor wife ever get over this? She removed her glasses and wiped the corners of her eyes. Sylvester felt greatly touched. Here was this nice Hindu lady weeping for poor Richie while his relatives secretly rejoiced at his death! Rejoiced because his status had again gone down with the boy's death. All of them were jealous of his son. He was so handsome and always wore such fashionable clothes. His penfriend in America had sent him through an air hostess two terylene shirts and a leather belt with the Beatles' songs written ever so nice in gold letters on its good side. His mom liked it so much. Now it is with his other things in an old trunk on the loft where Uncle Reggie's son hid it away so that mom will not see it and start weeping all over again.

You are a brave man, Mister Gomes, said the lady. He laughed. He looked into her tearful eyes. Don't you worry, Miss, he said. Such tragedies happen. The Good Lord knows what he is doing even if we don't. When I heard from the boys that Richie was drowned I ran out in the sun without my specs and also his mom without chappals in her old housecoat but the fishermen had already taken the body out and sent it to the city morgue. I went there to identify it. Without my specs, I am nearly blind, Miss. But a son is after all a son. I can identify him with my eyes shut. This is what I told the Inspector. The Coroner is a good chap. He could have created trouble for me. Everybody said, he would refuse to part with the body until all investigations are over. My master had of course given the Coroner a ring. He was at college in England with the Coroner's grandpop. They were thick pals then. So when I went to his room, the Coroner, he gives me a nod and says Mister Gomes, you may take your son's body without any delay. Yes, Miss I was really lucky.

14
IQBAL

One pineapple to lie at the side, and then the basket was ready. She had filled it with one layer of oranges, another of apples, and had spread over them pale green clusters of seedless grapes. In her handbag, she tucked in two bottles of cider wondering if anyone recovering from an overdose of sleeping pills would be allowed to drink any alcoholic stuff. And yet, the bottles had added the right touch, for after all the one who lay in the hospital was a poet, a minor, an unknown one perhaps, but a poet all the same.

> Your flesh was the flesh of the moon, dear love,
> But I was an orphan nurtured by the moon,
> I drank the white milk of the moon,
> And suckled her dry...

She recited Iqbal's short poem while she combed her long hair and tied it into a bun. What did he mean by those lines? She could never make out what her husband had found in the young man's verses to make him rave so over them. Meaningless, she said to herself, and wildly she stuck a pin into the knot of her hair. Now she was ready. Looking once again into the mirror she saw the bulge of her belly hidden by the shimmering silk and felt proud, suddenly.

Swinging her bag gaily with one arm, and holding the basket with the other, she went to the taxi stand.

In the hospital, Iqbal was lying with his eyes shut tight in a small room, and the nurse who ushered her in whispered, he is out of danger now, he will be discharged after a day or two.

She sat on a chair and deposited the basket on the floor. The white face visible over the whiter bedsheet looked pretty with its black curls, its full red lips and the nose that was delicately transparent. Iqbal should have been a girl, she thought, he would be such a hit with the young men. Then she remembered her husband's panic-stricken face and his voice telling her that Iqbal had taken poison and was in the hospital. It was only at that moment that she had first guessed the truth. During the days of their honeymoon, he had told her a lot about the young roommate of his YMCA days and had often recited his poems which were all about love. She had asked him if Iqbal was in love with any girl, and he had turned away, not answering. She had even then felt stabs of jealousy, but he had wrapped his pale white arms around her in a tight embrace and had made her quiet. How pale your arms are, she had cried in amazement when he had for the first time undressed before her. They have the luminescence of the moon...

When they had come to Bombay, there was Iqbal at Dadar station waiting for them, standing under the blue lamps of the platform, wearing a navy-blue shirt, but sullen, sullen, sullen, and she asked her husband, why doesn't he smile, this Iqbal, this great friend of yours. Iqbal avoided looking at her while he was being introduced. She walked slowly, allowing the men to go ahead of her, whispering, and anyway, the noise of the platform even at that hour was deafening. She was too busy watching the strange people to bother about her own husband and his young friend.

After a week when they had settled down, Iqbal was invited to spend a Sunday at their house but the poet stayed for only an hour and left, explaining that he had to meet an uncle who had fallen ill suddenly. Her husband walked with him to the railway station, and left her alone at home, wondering why he did not ask her to accompany them. Two days later, she found a poem under a mattress. Dear love, your flesh was the flesh of the moon but I was an orphan nurtured by the moon, I have drunk the white milk of the moon and have suckled her dry...

When Iqbal refused to come to their place for Sunday lunches her husband grew moody. You are a suspicious woman, he said one day without any cause. What is the matter with you, she asked him. Has anything gone wrong at the office? Why are you picking on me for nothing?

Her husband begged her to forgvie him. No, you are not at fault, he murmured. The fault is mine....What are you talking about, she asked him. I don't know what you are talking about.

As the baby grew inside her and bulged below her navel, her husband became a devoted lover. He wanted to keep his ears pressed to her belly, to hear baby's heart tick.

We shall name him Iqbal, she said, we shall please your friend that way. Her husband buried his head in her lap and for a minute she felt that he was sobbing.

When Iqbal was rushed to the hospital, her husband got a message from an uncle. Then there was such panic in the house. He went to sit beside the boy, and later, when he was out of danger, he came home and slept peacefully with his arm around her shoulder. When he had left for office, she had decided to visit Iqbal in the hospital. She had not consulted him...

Iqbal opened his eyes and she saw his eyes widening in fright. The boy is afraid of me, she thought with a feeling of triumph. I know why you did it, she said, Iqbal, I know why you did it. Iqbal did not speak. You are jealous of me, she continued. Why should I be jealous of you, asked the young man wearily. She smiled. You are jealous because it is not possible for you to become pregnant...She stood up revealing for one shimmering flash the convexity of her middle, and then she turned away to walk towards the door. Get out of here you devil, hissed Iqbal, and instead of growing angry she only felt her heart growing lighter, and laughter bubbling up inside her throat. She closed the door and the corridor rang with her laughter.

15

THE TATTERED BLANKET

When he reached his house in a jeep owned by the Government of India, unexpectedly one evening his old mother made an unsuccessful attempt to rise from her easy-chair.

Kamalam, who had come to our house, asked in a panic-stricken voice, just go out and see who has come.

The widowed daughter was seated on a ledge with a towel covering her head and cold ears and so most reluctantly she rose to walk up to the door and peer into the darkness outside.

A stout balding man was walking towards the porch.

Gopi? she asked him in a raucous voice, what kind of a visit is this, without writing about your coming?...

Who is it, Kamalam, asked the mother.

This is me, Mother, Gopi, said the man, I had to come to Trivandrum for a meeting and I thought I would motor down and stay the night here.

Who is this, Kamalam, who is this man, asked the mother again nervously.

Why are you getting so disturbed, *Amma*, this is only

Gopi, have you forgotten even your son Gopi, he is here to see you, said the widow.

The man bent forward to touch with his cheek his mother's wrinkled forehead.

Amma, this is me, your son Gopi, he said gently.

Gopi, what does this mean, asked the mother. Is the boy's school closed?

Mother is like this these days, said the sister. Occasionally, she forgets everything. Her mind blanks out. But sometimes she remembers only too clearly. Then she asks me why you have not written for such a long time. I tell her that you had written and that all of you are well. You, Vimala and the children. How can I tell her that you stopped writing a year ago? What is the use hurting mother's feelings?

Last year, I got a promotion, said the man, after that I have always been on the move. I hardly get any time to read or write.

You could have asked Vimala to write letters, said his sister, or is she as busy as yourself?

Who are you talking with, asked the old lady, who has come in a car?

Didn't I tell you, *Amma*, that it is Gopi, asked the younger woman.

Gopi? Is he not in Delhi, asked the mother.

Yes, *Amma*, I have just come from Delhi, the man said.

The old lady lowered her voice and asked her daughter, whom has he married?

Vimala. Don't you remember Vimala, the Collector's daughter, asked the sister of the man.

I forgot the name, said the mother apologetically, has he written to us this week, Kamalam?

Yes, his letters are regular, said the daughter.

When his letters get delayed, I feel wretched, said the old lady.

He knows it, said the daughter. That is why he writes every week.

Didn't I tell you how it was with her, asked Kamalam turning to her brother. But you are far away and probably don't care....

Who is standing here, asked the mother. Who is this man who has come by car?

This is me, your son Gopi. I came up to Trivandrum on official work and thought that....

Where does your mother live, asked the old lady. Is she anyone I know?

She lives close by, he said.

I can never explain things to Amma, said the sister in exasperation.

The man lifted his bag onto the ledge and opened it. It contained two shirts, a pair of terylene trousers, some pieces of underwear, his shaving kit and a few files.

Do you know Gopi, asked the old lady. He is in Delhi. He is a Government official. The astrologers told me that he has framed Kesari *yogam*. That is why he gets promotions so frequently. He gets two thousand and five hundred rupees every month. You must have surely heard of him.

Yes, I know him, said the man.

Please tell him that I want a new blanket, said the old mother, tell him that I cannot stand the cold in the mornings. When I catch a cold it does not leave me for at least a fortnight. Ask him to send me a blanket at once... A red blanket. I had one like that years ago. He had given it to me when he came home from his college hostel in Madras for the summer vacation. That was years ago. It got torn and tattered. I cannot use it any longer. It is now like a fisherman's net, it is of no use as a blanket. I want a new red blanket.

I will tell him, said the man.

Don't forget, reminded the old lady, the mornings are very cold. I am afraid of catching a cold. Let me go and lie down for a few minutes. I am tired. My back aches...

When the old lady had gone in to lie down, the man's sister turned to face him.

Why have you come, she asked him. It is not merely to see *Amma*, is it?

My expenses have increased, the man said, now I have four children and I can't make both ends meet. I have to maintain my status and live decently. I want to sell my share of the property and carry the money back to Delhi to put it in the fixed deposit. I came to discuss this matter with you.

You will sell your land and take leave of us. Then, we shall never be able to see you again, said the sister.

No, no, I shall come once a year to see *Amma*, he said. Whenever I get a chance to come to Kerala I shall look you up.

A chance to come to Kerala, exclaimed the widow, a sob rising in her throat. Is this not the first visit after five years? *Amma* is eighty Five years old. She is not likely to live much longer. How could you have stayed away from her for such a long time? What kind of a son are you, anyway?

But *Amma* does not remember me, he said with a laugh.

But did you remember your mother, asked his sister.

He did not answer.

16
LEUKAEMIA

When he brought his ten years old daughter home from the boarding school, he took his wife aside and said, do not ever weep in front of the child, she does not know the gravity of her illness.

Dear God, why are you punishing me so mercilessly, cried the mother, beating her own brow with a pale, beautiful hand. The man looked at her with distaste. She fully deserved the punishment, he told himself, forcing him to part with his only child when he had not had enough of her prattle, her slobbering kisses at night, her baby-smell....He was against sending a four-year-old to a boarding school so far away. It seemed so cruel to him and so stupid. But she gave him no peace until the child was taken to the fashionable boarding school and left there. At the beginning of each new year, he took a screaming child in his car to the railway station while the mother hid herself in the bedroom giving as an excuse her weak heart. After four years, the child stopped crying and stepped into the car with an adult stoicism that wrung his heart more than her tears. Returning home, he would always hear his wife remark that the boarding school had done the child a lot of good, taught her discipline and the method of eating neatly with forks and knives.

During one of the vacations the child said to her father, Papa, I am in a hurry to grow big.

What do you want to do when you grow big, asked the father.

When I grow big I shall be able to live with you and Mama, she said. At that moment, he hated his wife. He wanted to embrace the child and tell her that he wanted such a life as badly as she did, but he controlled his emotions and merely smiled.

When the letter arrived from the Mother Superior, he could not believe that his child was suffering from Leukaemia. Probably, the tests were wrong. Probably, she was pretending to be ill to be able to come home. But how did she fool the doctors?

When he lifted the child, all wrapped in a blanket, and placed her lightly on the backseat of the car, he realised all of a sudden that she had not fooled anybody. There was a darkness on her face that was not there before, a patina on the bronze of her skin. The nuns peered into the ear and whispered, we shall pray for you, dear...

When they reached home, the mother unlocked the show-case and took out the expensive toys to spread them out on the carpet. Play with all these toys, she said. What if they break, asked the child, mustering up the courage to touch them. Break them, they are yours, said the mother. Will you let me carry these to the boarding school when I go back, asked the child. The mother choked down a sob. We will not send you to the boarding school, she said, we will not send you back again....

Not even for the final exam in December, asked the little girl.

17
A DOLL FOR THE CHILD PROSTITUTE

It was the same old story. The stepfather raping the minor girl while her mother was out visiting her relatives. The fat woman called Ayee by the inmates of the house threw back her head and laughed aloud, displaying two rows of brown teeth resembling rusty nails. "Anasuya, what did you expect from a bum like your Govind?" she asked the thin visitor who had brought her twelve-year-old daughter for sale. "Anyway, let bygones be bygones. Stop worrying about this nice-looking girl of yours. She will be all right here. You will hardly recognize her after a couple of months. What she needs is good food. Look at my girls, Anasuya. Do you see any one of them looking unhealthy? I feed them eggs with their parathas in the morning." The little girl looked around. There were seven young women seated on the floor and all of them did look healthy. But peeping out of a window was a frail girl who wore orange bangles on her thin wrists. She could not have been more than fifteen. Perhaps she will be my friend, thought the little girl.

"Rukmani, come closer to me," said Ayee, drawing the child to her swollen bosom. "Take leave of your poor mother. She has a long way to go, and it is already late. The postman is returning home..."

"Any letter for me?" asked Ayee and the postman, slowing his bike, smiled good-humouredly at her.

"I am always hoping to hear from my beloved son, that good-for-nothing fellow who ran away from home ten years ago," said Ayee.

"You will hear from him," said the visitor, wiping a reddened nose on the corner of her saree. "Your heart is pure. God will not make you suffer long."

The child Rukmani looked at her mother with dry eyes. She was not unhappy about leaving her home. The man who had moved into her home some months ago, after her father had disappeared, was a monster. He not only beat up her mother every night but squeezed her own little breasts, hurting her dreadfully when she was alone in the house. And, last week he had pierced her body until she bled all over the floor.

"You ought not to have sent away the good man I married you off to, Anasuya," said Ayee. "He was a steady fellow and he never drank. But you lusted for a younger one. Are you satisfied now?"

"Do not taunt me so Ayee," pleaded Anasuya. "I have been a sinner. But please look after my child. She is innocent."

Anasuya rolled the dirty currency notes in a paper and tucked the roll into her waist. "I would not have taken any money from you, Ayee," she said, a sob rising in her throat, "but we are practically starving at home. The baby is given nothing but tea and may be a banana at noon."

When she left the place and walked towards the bus stop, the child Rukmani watched her, leaning against the bars of the porch. Finally, when her mother resembled a tiny green spot and dissolved with the other colours in the distance, she turned back to look at her new mother. Ayee was kneading lime and tobacco in the palm of her left hand. The thin girl emerged from the interior and smiled at Rukmani, crinkling her eyes. She was wearing a blue skirt and a torn white blouse. The bangles on her wrists had a frosted look.

"Do you wish to have some of these?" asked the thin girl. "They are nylon bangles, not plastic. Ayee bought them for me at the fair last month."

"Sita, you must teach Rukmani the customs of this place," said Ayee. "She is two years younger than you."

Sita held Rukmani by her waist. "You can have my bangles," she said, looking at the child's wrists. Then she gave a laugh. "Oh, you are big-made, aren't you?" Sita asked Rukmani. Rukmani's hands were large compared to Sita's pale ones. She felt clumsy all of a sudden. "Orange will not suit a dark skin," said Rukmani. "You are not dark," said Ayee. "You have been walking to your school in the hot sun and that is why you have such a tan. We shall make you fair skinned in a month's time."

A dark woman lying curled up on the floor, got up and glared at the child. "What is wrong in being dark?" she asked Ayee. "I am dark, but every client asks for me..."

Sita dragged Rukmani into the corridor of the house which was dark and had a steamy smell. Then she was taken to a hall where on reed-mats, some young women were sleeping. One of them was wearing only a short skirt which had slipped up to reveal the cheeks of her buttocks. Rukmani looked away in disgust. "Oh this one, she is utterly shameless," said Sita throwing a towel over the sleeping woman's legs. "She is Radha. She has a bad temper. So be careful when you deal with her." Sita pointed to a mat in the corner of the hall. "That is where I sleep in the day," she said. "You may share the mat with me."

"I cannot sleep in the day," said Rukmani.

Sita laughed loudly and held on to her stomach as though it was about to burst. "You are a baby," she said. "You are so innocent. Do you think we can sleep at night in this house? We shall all be so busy entertaining the visitors."

"Visitors at night?" asked Rukmani. "Who will come at night?"

Sita could not control her laughter. "Oho ho," she laughed, "you are too funny, you will make me piss in my skirt..."

Rukmani kept her satchel of books on the mat meant for her and Sita. "Men come to do things here," said Sita.

"What things?" asked Rukmani. She was thinking of her stepfather and the pain she had experienced when he climbed her on the floor.

"You will find out soon enough," said Sita. "Obey them or else Ayee will starve you to death. Do whatever they want you to do. Men are real dogs."

Then they tiptoed out into the corridor while a soft voice asked them from inside a room, "Who is it?" "It is me, Sita," said the pale girl. "Don't make too much noise," chided the soft voice.

"That is Mirathai, the favourite of this house," said Sita in a whisper. "Ayee has given her a room all to herself. She is a beautiful woman. And she is a matriculate, not like the rest of the gang who are all uneducated. How far have you studied, Rukmani?"

"I am in the sixth standard," said Rukmani.

"That is good enough," said Sita. "You must be able to read English, just a little?"

"Not English," said Rukmani. "English is tough. We started it only this year. I can read Marathi and Hindi."

"Then you must read out a book a client left for me to read. It contains dirty pictures of naked men and women. I pretended that I was educated and so he gave that book to me." Saying this, Sita laughed again.

"Why do you hold your stomach when you laugh?" asked Rukmani.

"When I laugh I get a queasy feeling inside my belly," Sita said. "I am not too well these days. I have even lost my appetite."

From the porch, rose a strident voice in protest. "No, no, that is not true, Lachmi," it said. "I will never speak against your girls. You are like a younger sister to me. Besides, what can I say against your girls? Everybody knows that you keep a disciplined house and that your girls are plump and healthy. The Inspector Saheb told me that your Mira resembled a filmstar who has become of late very famous. I cannot recollect the name. It is a lengthy fashionable name."

Ayee spread out her fat legs and leaned against the wall. She chewed the tobacco pensively for a minute. "Where did you meet the Inspector Saheb, Sindhuthai?" she asked the visitor. The old woman took a pinch of tobacco from Ayee's betel box and pretended not to hear. Ayee repeated the question. Sindhuthai knew what a loaded question it was. "I met him at Koushalya's place yesterday," said Sindhuthai.

"The ingrate," shouted Ayee. "Here I give him expensive gifts and every week his *hafta* of fifty rupees and all the girls free, and he has the audacity to go to my rival's house for his quota of fun. What is wrong with my children? Are Koushalya's girls as clean as mine? Filthy, five rupeewalis."

"Don't get upset, younger sister," said Sindhuthai.

"Inspector Saheb said he was tired of women. He wanted little girls."

"We don't have little girls," asked Ayee. "What about Sita? Is she not lovely with her white skin and petite figure?"

"Sita is not cooperative any longer he said," whispered the hag.

"Have you seen the child I have bought today?" asked Ayee. "Rukmani, come here and let Sindhuthai see you."

Sita pushed Rukmani into the porch. The old woman pinched the child's calves and stroked her posterior. "Yes, she is firm and sweet," said Sindhuthai. "How much did you pay for her? She must have cost you a lot of money."

Ayee whispered something into the old woman's ear. "Oh she is our Anasuya's child," Sindhuthai said, "that is why she has such beautiful legs."

"Will you tell the Inspector Saheb that we have this little Goddess in our house?" asked Ayee.

"Yes, I shall do so this very evening," said Sindhuthai. She took some betel from the brass box and turned to go. Her gnarled hands with their dirty talons frightened the little girl. When the hag was staring at her, she had felt that a woodpecker was pecking at her skin. "What an odious creature," she murmured to Sita.

"Yes", said Sita, "she is a scandalmonger. I hate her."

II

All the street lights were on but the sky was still grey when Mirathai's client, the college student, walked in with a swagger, calling out imperiously, "Mira, Mira." Ayee was still in the bathroom having her legs massaged with mustard oil but she heard his voice and frowned. "It is that talkative swain again," she remarked to the girl who was at her feet. "If he does not pay this time, I shall get the police to throw him out," continued Ayee. "Radha, has he been to you any time?"

"No," said Radha, "he wants only Mira. He behaves as if he is her husband. He talks to her half the night and even quarrels."

"Half the night?" asked Ayee. "Does he pay for such a long session?"

"Don't ask me," said Radha. "After all Mira is your pet. None can question her in this house. She has begun to be fastidious of late. She refused even the Inspector Saheb yesterday complaining that she had a headache. She does not behave like a prostitute. She wants to be faithful to her college student..."

"Don't use such coarse terms, Radha," said Ayee.

"You do not like the word *prostitute*," muttered Radha, "but you know well that all of us are prostitutes. I believe in being frank and truthful."

"Rub my knee harder," said Ayee.

From Mira's closed room rose the rumble of a male voice.

Mira laughed once.

Ayee was disturbed. "What is he always talking about?" asked Ayee.

"He is teaching her politics," said Radha.

"He is impotent, is he?" asked Ayee.

"I do not know, Ayee," said the girl. "He does not touch any of us. All I know is that he leaves Mira always with a headache. After he has visited her, she refuses to entertain any client. She sits on her bed humming strange tunes." Ayee got up and walked towards the closed door. The

73

young man was still talking briskly and Ayee could only pick out certain words which were familiar. Once or twice, he mentioned the word "revolution". Ayee knocked on the door. "Who is it?" asked Mira. "Open the door, "said Ayee. Mira opened the door. She was wearing her green saree and on the bed which still had an uncrumpled sheet, sat the student, smoking.

"Do you come all the way here to tell her of a revolution?" asked Ayee.

The youth coloured. "I have paid the money," he said. Ayee looked at him with contempt. "This is a brothel," she said, "not a conference hall. Get on with your job and get out," added Ayee. "Other clients will be coming in a few minutes' time."

The door was shut again. Ayee went up to the porch and surveyed the scene. The girls were wearing clothes sparkling with *jari* and sequins. They had make-up on their faces and flowers in their hair. The two young ones were playing with bits of tiles on a large diagram chalked out on the floor. "Stop this childish game, Sita," ordered Ayee. "The clients are about to arrive."

At that precise moment, the Inspector who was a burly man entered the porch and pointing to Rukmani asked: "Is this your new recruit?" Ayee nodded. "Come in," said the man dragging the child into the interior.

"Go child, he is our friend," said Ayee.

The Inspector threw the child on a charpoy and lifted her frock. "You wear underpants like girls of the upper classes," said the man, laughing. Rukmani felt his hands on her and struggled to get free. "Let me go," she cried, "if you don't, I shall scratch your eyes out."

"What did you say, you wild cat?" asked the angry man. His voice underwent a change, and became very hoarse. "You will scratch me, will you, little whore..."

"I am not a whore," cried Rukmani. But the man did not care to listen. He was panting as though he had run a race and there was froth at the corners of his wide mouth. Later, he turned over and closed his eyes. "I shall buy you a red frock," he whispered, "and panties with lace on them."

Rukmani rose from the bed and ran back to the porch. Her hair was tousled and sweat beaded her brow. But she began once again to hop in the squares of the diagram while Sita watched animatedly. "I have won," cried Rukmani a little while later in triumph. Just then, the Inspector came out of the room and gave Ayee a slow smile.

"She is a vixen, all right. Knows the tricks of the trade. I liked her immensely."

Rukmani glanced at the man whose face was red with the scratches inflicted by her own nails. He looked complacent.

"Who is prattling away in Mira's room?" asked the Inspector.

Ayee beat her head in mock anguish: "It is that student again, come to teach her politics."

"I can drive him out of this place," said the Inspector, "only give me a day's notice. I can even get him arrested and sent to jail."

"I know you can," said Ayee. "But let us wait until Mira tires of him. Mira is like my daughter. I love her dearly. I don't wish to hurt her feelings."

"You have spoilt her already, Lachmibai," said the Inspector. "She behaves as if she is well born."

"Who can say for certain that she is not well-born?" asked Ayee. "When I found her at my doorstep, she was wrapped in an expensive silk saree, not the kind worn by people of our station."

"Her mother must have been a maid working for a rich woman who gave that saree to her for Diwali or some such function," said the man reaching for Ayee's betel box.

"She certainly does not look like a poor woman's child," said Ayee. "Whenever I take the girls out to the town for shopping, people stare at her with hungry eyes. If my lost son were to return, I shall certainly marry her off to him. They will make a fine couple. Both are fair skinned, and both have light eyes."

"Is your son's father a Chitpavan Brahmin?" asked the Inspector and both he and the old woman laughed in mirth. "I must get going," said the man.

"Is it true that you have started to visit Koushalya's place?" asked Ayee. "Do not leave my place without giving me a truthful answer."

"I shall get that witch Sindhuthai arrested and sent to jail," said the man. "She must have seen me walk past that house yesterday towards the bus stop, and she did not waste time in passing the information to you. Why should I go to that house, Lachmibai?"

Ayee blew out her nose and looked as if she was about to cry. "That Koushalya, she spreads such horrible tales about my innocent girls," said Ayee. "Sindhuthai said that she was telling people that my girls were diseased. What will happen to our business if such stories are circulated. My poor girls will starve to death."

"Don't cry," said the Inspector, sheepishly stroking the woman's plump hand. "I shall protect your reputation. I am your friend. I shall never let you down."

Ayee brightened up a little. She even attempted a smile. "Take some *paan*, Inspector Saheb," she whispered.

After the Inspector had left, Ayee slipped into a sullen mood. She began to taunt her girls who were looking out through the bars. "What is wrong with all of you," she asked, "have you forgotten how to attract men? I waste my money buying eggs and dalda and fish for all of you but not one of you know how to hold onto a man except that Mira and now she has latched on to a good-for-nothing fellow who teaches her politics. How many important people pass this way in their cars, slowing down as they pass this way to be able to see you and yet you do not do a thing to lure them in. What a bunch of pigs, I have reared here. Koushalya is far more fortunate than I am. She whips her girls but that has only done them good. Look at the cars that have stopped near her place. Two already and it is not yet eight o'clock. I am going to throw you all out and go to Benaras. Let me at least die in peace..."

The dark girl called Saraswati climbed down the porch and gestured to a young man who was watching out from a bus. Within a few minutes the young man was at her side, having got off at the next bus stop. She took him into the corridor, swinging her full hips and walking ahead of him. Ayee rubbed her eyes with the edge of her saree.

"I don't do these things because it is crude," said the girl called Radha. "I hate to stand out and solicit like a common streetwalker." Then someone came asking for Sita. "Ayee, not tonight," begged Sita, wanting to be let off.

"Go with him, child," said Ayee, pushing Sita gently beyond the doorway.

"Rukmani, do not remove my piece from that square," cried Sita. "I shall be back to finish the game. He is a kind man, although a Madrasi," said Ayee. "He is working in a school. Comes during the first week of every month and only selects Sita. He has three grown-up daughters studying in college. His wife is stricken with Arthritis. He tells me all about his life. He does not hide anything. He is not secretive like the others..."

Ayee heard the sound of a woman's weeping from inside the house. She listened in silence for a moment or two. "Is that our Mira weeping?" she asked. "Go and see what is happening inside her room. Men are odd creatures. One cannot predict their actions. When I was young, a rich man came to me and whipped me for half an hour and went his way paying me thirty rupees. In those days, thirty was a large sum of money. I was too astonished to cry. I used to wait for him but he never turned up again."

"What was your son's father like, Ayee?" asked Radha.

Ayee got up and gave a friendly slap on her cheek. "Don't you dare talk about the father of my son," said Ayee. "He was a Brahmin. He was not like any of the men who come here to see all of you. He was a wise man. He used to recite the scriptures while dressing up to go."

"He sounds so much like our Mirathai's friend," said Radha. "He sings the Gitagovinda to her on some nights. I have heard her trying to sing the songs that he has taught her."

"Mira has a sweet voice," said Ayee. "She is a gem of a girl. I wonder who left her on my doorstep nineteen years ago? Perhaps it was some high-born woman who had conceived while her husband was away."

"Perhaps it was some harlot who did not want to be saddled with a baby," said Radha.

"All of you are jealous of Mira," said Ayee.

Just then Mira's client walked out without looking back even once. Ayee sat up in surprise. He looked as if he had been weeping too. What was wrong with the young man? Was he mentally inbalanced? She decided to speak to Mira about him. I would not do to encourage such an eccentric. Mira ought to try and bait a man of substance, a businessman who is tired of his wife or a politician who craves for relaxation off and on, someone who can bring her expensive gifts and bestow on the house a certain prestige.

"Mira," Ayee called out to the weeping girl, "come out this minute." Mira came out and stood under the neon lamp, moon-coloured and slender. Only her eyes made large by collyrium looked red. "What has he done to you, my daughter?" asked Ayee.

"He did nothing, Ayee," said Mira. "He is always kind to me."

"What made you weep?" asked the old woman. "He must have said something to upset you." Mira looked down at her feet. She did not reply.

"Did he call you names?" asked Ayee.

"No, Ayee," said Mira, "he said that he had to sell his pen to visit me. He has no income of his own. He comes here saving his lunch-allowance and his bus fare. He loves me..." Mira's eyes filled with tears.

III

When Sita vomited all over the floor of the room and scared her client away, Ayee was very angry with her. The man had asked for a refund of the money he had paid Ayee and had as a parting shot exclaimed that the house was full of diseased whores. Ayee entered the room to find Sita seated on the floor with vomit all round her and making a loud sound while she struggled to bring out more from her stomach. Her eyes were wide with fear Ayee pulled her by her long braid and slapped her hard on her face. "You have ruined the reputation of this house," said Ayee. "You eat all kinds of dirty things sold by the street vendors and throw up into the faces of our clients. How many times have I told you never to eat pani-puri or bhel? Ungrateful girl. I will see that you starve for three days."

Sita began to weep: "Ayee, it is not my fault," she whimpered. "I have not been feeling well for the past few days. I cannot eat anything. I feel a heart-burn in the evenings..."

"You have lost some weight," said Ayee. Then she lifted the girl's white blouse and peered at her tiny breasts. "It is not possible," murmured Ayee. "You have not even attained puberty."

Sita was given three days' leave. She was overjoyed. "I do not have to attend to any man for three days," she cried out in a voice thinkened with happiness. "We shall play hopscotch with bits of tiles, Rukmani, for hours and hours."

Leaning against the bars of the porch, Sita said to her friend: "Look at the sky this afternoon, it is like a whitewashed wall. Once upon a time I lived in a house with white walls. Every year during Diwali, my father whitewashed our walls with lime and powdered sand."

"Where is your father?" asked Rukmani. Sita shrugged her shoulders. "He is dead. All are dead. Cholera got them all four years ago. There were five deaths in my family. My father, my mother, my three brothers..."

"But what happened to that house with the white walls?" asked Rukmani.

"That must have died too," said Sita laughing.

"Everything dies, Rukmani. Even the sky." Rukmani looked up at the blanched brilliance of the sky. It hurt her eyes.

Ayee called the young girls to her side in the afternoon. "Come, let me do your hair for you," she said. First, it was Rukmani's turn. Ayee removed the snarls from her curly hair and plaited it tight. Rukmani wrinkled her face in discomfort. "I shall get you Brahmani oil for your hair," said Ayee. "Then in two months' time, it will have more body. Your hair is too soft and silky. Sita's is thick enough. In fact, she is too weak to carry the burden of her hair."

While their hair was being done, Sindhuthai climbed up the steps beside the porch, rubbing gratingly her rough feet on the stone. She cleared her throat and said: "How are you today, my younger sister, you look happy today."

Ayee grew pale at the thought of the hag's evil eye. "We are pulling on, thanks to the blessings of Lord Ganesh," said Ayee. "Sita here is not too well. She has lost her appettite for food."

"Has she attained puberty?" asked Sindhuthai.

"No" said Ayee. "Otherwise, I would not have been so thoroughly upset. I am wondering if I should take her to the doctor sabeb today."

"Don't you take your girls to the doctor sabeb every week?" asked Sindhuthai. It was another of her loaded questions.

Ayee squirmed in embarrassment. "Why do you ask such a question?" she asked the old woman. "Has that bitch Koushalya been telling you that I do not get my girls medically checked up every week?"

"Yes, that was what she told me yesterday," said Sindhuthai. "I was passing by her house on my way to the ration shop when she stopped me. She insisted on my going in, to take a glass of tea with her. How could I refuse the offer and incur her displeasure? You know well what a lot of mischief, she is capable of when her ire is aroused. Koushalya will make a deadly foe for anyone who irritates her. She has of late become very influential too. I saw the car of a high Government official parked near her place."

"How does she manage it," asked Ayee, "with her scummy bunch of girls?"

"They are well-trained," said the hag.

"I am taking my girls this very minute to the doctor saheb's dispensary," said Ayee. "I am sorry I cannot sit here talking to you, Sindhuthai."

"I understand, sister," said the hag, picking up shreds of tobacco from the box. "I am feeling weak and dizzy today," said Sindhuthai. "Younger sister, have you any money you can spare for a soda? Soda settles my stomach each time I feel ill."

"Sindhuthai, you don't mean soda, do you?" asked Ayee. "You drink country liquor whenever you can lay your hands on it. The Inspector Saheb himself told me that he saw you buy a bottle of *moosambi*."

"Scandalmongers all over the place," cried out the hag. "Everybody hates me nowadays. In my time, I have helped all of you in many ways. Now nobody loves me. All make fun of me. When youth goes away every wowan becomes an object of ridicule. Lachmi, you have a house now, but watch my words, after another ten years you will be thrown out from here like a rind and another will become the Ayee of this place. Most probably Mira. Or that dark one Saraswati."

"Don't say such things with your accursed tongue, Sindhuthai," cried out Ayee. "My girls will always love me. I have never ill-treated them. Ask Rukmani here. Ask them all how I have fed them, and how I have nursed them with my own hands during illness. They will not throw me out as your girls once threw you out, Sindhuthai. I will be their Ayee until my death."

Sindhuthai chortled sarcastically: "This is what I too thought once upon a time, Lachmi," she said, "but see what happened. My favourite girls threw me out calling me names. What could I do? I was past the age for attracting any man. All I could do was roam around looking for a hut to live in, a shelter over my head. I begged at street corners for a year. Then I became a useful member of this locality. I could perform abortions for as little as twenty rupees. So you invited me into your houses. I was lucky. But how can you be sure that you will be as lucky as I have been?"

Ayee hid her round dark face in the folds of her saree and wept unashamedly. Sita remembered the gurgling sound the buffaloes made while they wallowed in the muddy pools of her village. How funny Ayee's sobs sounded. She nudged Rukmani with an elbow. She wanted suddenly to giggle. But Rukmani was watching the fat woman cry, intently and with a sympathetic expression on her face.

Mira called out from inside: "Rukmani, come here for a minute. I cannot hook my choli which is open at the back."

Rukmani went inside to help Mira who was standing dressed only in a satin petticoat of black and an open choli. She looked radiantly happy. She had a red spot of *sindoor* on her brow and *kajal* in her eyes: "Mirathai, are you going out anywhere?" asked the little girl.

"Oh, no, I am dressing to meet my friend who is coming this evening," said Mira.

"You look like a married woman," said the girl and Mira embraced her with a sudden laugh.

"I am married," said Mira, "but don't tell anybody about it..."

"Are you married to the student who visits you," asked Rukmani, "the one who sold his fountain pen to come to you?"

"Yes, he is my husband. He is called Krishna. Is that not strange, Rukmani?" Mira asked the little girl. "Is it not strange that I am Mira and he is Krishna?"

Rukmani remained silent. She felt Mirathai was behaving peculiarly that evening. It was like the delirium of those who have high fever. There was a red flush on her high cheek bones and a glitter in her eyes. Mira decorated her hair with a string of mogra flowers and bit her lips to make them redder. "Why don't you use some lipstick?" asked Rukmani.

"He does not like lipstick," said Mira.

When Rukmani had finished hooking her choli, Mira hugged her with passion and kissed her forehead. "God bless you, my child," said Mira.

When she went out in the porch, Ayee had stopped her crying and Sindhuthai had vanished. Rukmani sat on the steps near Sita who was watching the buses go by. "One day, Ayee took us in a double-decker bus," said Sita. "Then I put out my hand and plucked a guava from a tree."

"Your are a liar," said Rukmani.

"Ask Ayee," whispered Sita. "I plucked a ripe guava from the tree. I ate it on the bus. It was full of seeds. I liked the seeds the best of all. Ayee said that the guava seeds produce worms in the stomach. Long wriggly worms."

"Maybe you have such worms in your stomach," said Rukmani. "That is why you threw up last night..."

"I threw up because I cannot any longer stand being messed up by men. I hate all of them."

"Don't you want to get married?" asked Rukmani. "Don't you want a home of your own and a few children?"

"Yes, I would love to have a home of my own and a few children. I want a plump baby to dandle on my knee. I want him to smile at me and call me Ma. But I don't want to have any man in my house."

A client entered hiding his face from the passersby. "You are very early," said Ayee, "it is not yet evening."

"I am busy in the evening," said the man. He wore a white bushshirt and terylene trousers which looked dirty. He looked around him nervously and bit his nails.

"All right, make your choice," said Ayee gesturing towards the group of girls. Except for Mira, all were seated on the porch. Radha was as usual showing a lot of her things sitting in a careless posture. The man signalled to her and she rose obediently to escort him indoors.

From Mira's room rose the lilting tune of Jayadeva's Gitagovinda. "Mira sings beautifully," said Ayee.

The girls listened in silence.

Ratisukha sare gathamabhi sare madana manohara vesham.

Nakuru nithabini gamanavilambhana manusarathum hridayesham Radhe!

IV

It was only towards the morning that Ayee discovered that Mira had eloped with the college student. Mira's room was shut and the other girls knocked on the door casually while passing, calling out: "Mirathai, did he leave you so exhausted that you cannot even get up from your bed?" There was no angry answer, no light laughter. "Come and eat your breakfast," cried Radha knocking hard at the door. Breakfast was served at six every morning, a heavy meal of parathas dripping with vanaspati and an egg curry. There was a glass of milk to top the meal. After partaking of this meal the girls normally curled up on their mats and fell asleep until it was time again for the next meal which was at two. It was only after five that they stirred themselves to attend to their toilet. The bath was elaborate and afterwards their hair was decked with strings of flowers, and, rouge was rubbed into the skin of their cheeks to make them look healthy. Beneath the pink powder the bare skin was ashen and seemed to have aged prematurely. Using their bodies as rinds had killed their spirits. Only the young children, Rukmani and Sita, laughed normally. But they hardly knew the significance of the sexual act. For them, it came as an occasional punishment meted out for some obscure reason.

Perhaps the mistake they committed was that they got born as girls in a society that regarded the female as a burden, a liability. The two girls resented the frequent interruptions during their game of squares and even while the coarse men, old enough to be their grandfathers, took the pleasure off their young bodies, the children's minds were far away, hopping in the large squares of the chalked diagram on the floor of the porch.

When Radha pushed open the door, she found Mira's room empty except for the bed that was not slept in. Her tin-trunk, containing the coloured sarees she was fond of wearing, had disappeared. On the window sill lay a cracked mirror, as small as Mira's palm, and some sindoor, spilt on the edge. "Where has our Mirathai gone?" asked Radha clutching at her own brow. "Has she run away with that crazy student of hers?" Ayee sat on Mira's bed and wept with a great deal of emotion. "My golden bird has flown out of her cage" she wailed while from outside the window a crow cawed rapidly as though it had also heard the shocking news, and was perturbed. Radha smoothed Ayee's hair and spoke soothing words. "She is sure to return," she said. "That fellow has no money with him. After they have sold Mirathai's gold chain and have lived off its price they will come back to beg for food." Still Ayee continued with her wailing which rose higher, higher, until the neighbours rushed in to seek the cause of her grief. Koushalya was the first to arrive. "What has happened, elder sister?" she asked Ayee.

"My Mira has been kidnapped by my enemies," said Ayee. "All were jealous of her beauty. All the high Government officials came asking for her. And rich businessmen. Now I am lost. There is no girl here who can lure in men the way my Mira could. What a golden skin she had. What a body. I shall go to Benares this week and die there."

"Mira must have gone willingly," said Koushalya. "Such things have happened before, and in the best of houses. Didn't that Nepali girl fly the coop last year from Marine Drive? Let her go and perish. You must not upset yourself about an ungrateful girl."

"You know how I looked after the girls here, Koushalya?" asked Ayee. "I used to give them parathas made in ghee, eggs, milk, and cod-liver-oil tablets. I used to take them to all the *melas* and the exhibitions going on in the city. I loved them deeply..."

"Elder sister, you are too kind," said Koushalya. "I have been wanting to warn you about being overkind to these girls. Kindness does not beget kindness. I whip them whenever they make a mistake and so they fear me. My girls are docile. They will not play hopscotch on the porch all through the afternoon like your young ones. You know that it is illegal to subject minors to a life of prostitution, don't you? People are beginning to talk about your house. People who are your so-called friends. I shall not mention their names."

"Who talked about my girls?" asked Ayee, rising from Mira's bed, with red eyes. "Was it that witch Sindhuthai? Was it the Inspector Saheb?"

Koushalya shook her head enigmatically and smiled. "I did not come here to gossip," she said. "I wanted only to comfort you."

Ayee embraced Koushalya with a new-found affection. "You are kind to me," she said. "We should stick together," said Koushalya. "We have common enemies. If we are united none can harm us, not even the police..."

The dark girl Saraswati immediately moved her things into Mira's room. "I get more clients than anyone else," she said in explanation. "I have always had an eye on this room. This looks out on the wide street. I can sit at the window-sill and charm the men who go about in motor cars."

Radha sulked. But she could not afford to argue with Saraswati who brought in an income higher than hers. "She is common," she murmured in another's ear, "have you seen how she swings her fleshy hips, this way, that way, when any man is looking at her?...."

Ayee kept whining about the ingratitude of Mira, seated on the charpoy in the porch while the labourers and the mill-hands walked past nonchalantly. When the Inspector came in, it was past noon, and he asked her incredulously, "Lachmi bai, why did you not inform me earlier?" Ayee beat a slow tattoo on her dark forehead and continued wailing monotonously. "If I had known of this earlier, I would have brought back the erring wench by now," the Inspector said. "I would have had my men to comb the railway platform and the bus stops and would have by now sent that rogue to our jail. Now they must be far away from the city, probably in some village trying to find work."

"What is the use trying to jail the boy?" asked Ayee. "Mira went willingly. She is not a minor either. Rukmani told me that Mira had secretly married the boy."

"Marriage," shouted the Inspector. "Why would a decent boy marry a prostitute? He will set up practice as a pimp and earn money from her. Lachmi bai, you are much too innocent to guess the ways of this shrewd world. That hussy refused to let me touch her; do you know that? One day, I offered her thirty rupees and yet she said 'No Inspector Saheb, I cannot be unfaithful to the man I love.' Is that the way a girl from a decent brothel like yours talks to an influential man like me? I could have thrashed her then and there with my cane but I did not want to create a ruckus in your house. You are like my elder sister, Lachmi bai."

"You speak the truth, Inspector Saheb," cried Ayee. "You are my brother. In times of distress, I look to you for guidance. Without your help, I would not have flourished in this locality. I often wonder why I cannot take my girls and move to a better locality, the Grant Road or Colaba for instance. My girls have class, don't they? My little moppet Rukmani has charmed every client who has come here. She has such a supple body, such a clean smell. Inspector Saheb, she was telling me yesterday that she liked you immensely. She called you a handsome man."

"Where is the girl?" asked the man, trying to peer into the darkness of the corridor. "She must be lying asleep in the hall," said Ayee. "She wept the most when Mira disappeared. Mira used to bathe her in the mornings and sing songs to her."

"May I see Rukmani for a few minutes?" asked the man.

Ayee went inside to call the little girl and found her playing with two plastic dolls, dressing them up to look like a wedded pair. Sita lay on the floor, sideways, watching her.

"The Inspector Saheb wishes to see you child," whispered Ayee to Rukmani. "Leave your dolls and go to the little room next to mine. I shall send him there..."

"Ayee, not now," protested the child. "We are playing a game just now. We are about to marry our doll off to the new doll bought yesterday. We have named them Mira and Krishna. Please ask that horrid man to go away."

Ayee bent down and tweaked her ear. "Get up this very minute," she said. "You cannot afford to displease the Inspector Saheb. He is a very important man. If he wants you now you must go and please him. I do not want disobedience from you."

"All right, Ayee," said the girl, rising slowly from the floor. "Wait for me, Sita, I shall be back in a short while to complete the wedding ceremony." Sita smiled wanly, still lying on the floor.

The Inspector Saheb was very gentle with the young girl. "Do you want me to buy you a doll that opens and closes its eyes?" he asked her, fondling her chubby arms. "Yes," said Rukmani. "There is such a doll in a shop at Churchgate," said the man. "It cries 'Mummy' when you press it on its stomach. It is a foreign doll. It costs about hundred rupees. But I do not mind spending the money on you if you are kind to me off and on. I love you more than I love anyone else in this world."

'What about your wife and children?" asked the child.

"I do not love them the way I love you, Rukmani," he said. "I have a granddaughter of your age, but even her I cannot love the way I love you. I will get you toys every month if you promise to remain kind to me. I am not good looking like that student who carried Mira away but I have a soft heart inside me. I am ugly. I am like a monkey, am I not? Do you feel an urge to laugh at me when you see my face?"

Rukmani felt moved by the man's humility. "You are not ugly," she said. "You are a little bit like my father who left us and went away. Whenever I see you I remember him."

"You will never be unhappy again in your life, my darling," cried the Inspector. "I shall protect you. I shall ask Lachmi bai to keep you away from all clients except myself. You can be my keep. I shall pay her a fixed sum of money so that she will not complain. Will you like that arrangement?"

"But what will happen when some young man comes forward and asks me to marry him?" asked the girl.

"I shall be that young man, my mogra flower,"

whispered the man hoarsely, holding her tight.

Rukmani felt a slight nausea when she was assailed by the mouldy smell of his scalp where white hair grew in untidy patches. But she closed her eyes immediately and lay passive, thinking of the foreign doll that cost hundred rupees.

V

When Rukmani saw Sindhuthai go into the little room next to Ayee's with a lump of green paste, resembling ground *mehndi* leaves and a sharp stick, she had a sense of foreboding. Sita had already been taken to the room, Ayee dragging her by her thin arms, while the child cried out, "No, no Ayee, I do not want that hag to touch me." The door was locked from within but Rukmani stood near the door trying to listen to the sounds from inside. She could hear Sindhuthai's shrill voice chiding Sita and then the girl's slow whimper. Later, there was a shriek which was muffled midway by somebody's rough hands. Rukmani felt her legs weaken. What were they doing to her friend, Sita?

Rukmani walked over to the bars of the porch and looked out. A double-decker bus rumbled along the road carrying in it men who stared at her. The sky was once again like a newly whitewashed wall. She remembered what Sita had told her of the little house in the village where five deaths took place in a month. Then at that precise moment she heard the scream which did not sound like a human voice at all. Was it some kind of a beast that had escaped from the zoo, she wondered. After a few minutes, Sindhuthai came out and quietly sat herself down on Ayee's charpoy. She picked up a drying leaf from the betel box and began to chew. "Our Sita is in a grave condition," she said. "I think she may even die."

Rukmani ran into the house. The door of the small room was half open. Ayee and Radha were tucking old sarees between Sita's thighs. Blood was soaking through the clothes rapidly. Sita lay insensate like a doll. How pale she looked with the rash of the midday sun mottling her narrow face. She resembled a foreign doll. Only her belly seemed alive, protruding from her flat body like a growth. Would she utter `Mummy' when she was pressed on her tummy, like that expensive doll? "Rukmani, our Sita is going away," sighed Ayee, speaking in a soft voice. "She is going to paradise where all the good people go after death." "Is Sita dying?" asked Rukmani. None answered.

The Inspector was very helpful during the next few hours. He brought the Doctor to write down the medical report, and after another hour, the body was taken to the electric crematorium and burnt down to ash in the presence of Ayee and three of the older girls. What remained of Sita was only a plastic doll bought from a street hawker, a light green male doll which was named Krishna by Rukmani and was married to the other doll. Rukmani lay between the two dolls in the evening, shedding tears in silence. When a client knocked at the door, Radha whispered to him: "Please go away today, we have had a tragedy at the house this morning," and he left without much protest.

That night Rukmani woke up to hear a male voice coming from Saraswati's room. Saraswati's period of mourning did not last long. Rukmani felt all of a sudden a need for emotional security. If only Ayee put an arm around her shoulders and comforted her, she would sleep well again. She felt the presence of Sita in the room. If only the Inspector Saheb could come and take her to the little room and tell her that he loved her more than all...

The next morning, Ayee called an astrologer to the house. He drew a diagram on the floor and spread out some cowries in each of the squares. "You are certainly passing through an unfavourable *dasa* in your life," he said. "You said that a girl eloped from here with a client and that another girl died. More calamities will follow, if you do not do a puja to control the evil stars who are your enemies."

"Stars are my enemies," asked Ayee. "Even stars have turned against me. I have several enemies in this locality. All are jealous of me. I shall not of course mention names. I was planning to move to a better place, Marine Drive or Pasta Lane in Colaba. Would that give me peace of mind?"

"Getting a new place will cost you a fortune. The *pugree* itself will be a lakh," said the astrologer. "This place is well located. All you need to do is a *havan* which will cost you only a thousand at the most. All your foes will be wiped out. Your business will thrive."

"Can you find someone to do it for me?" asked Ayee.

The astrologer glanced with lewd eyes at the girls lounging around on the porch. "I shall myself perform it," he said. "But it has to be done in secret. Is there a back verandah in this house?"

After the astrologer left, Sindhuthai arrived to comfort Ayee. "It is God's will, younger sister," she said. "Otherwise why would such a young girl become pregnant? She had not even attained her puberty. Such a thing is unheard of. Sita was not destined to live long. She had all the signs of one who is to die early in life. Don't you remember her pale lips? Her frail wrists?"

Ayee began to weep. "She was such an affectionate girl," said Ayee. "She used to prepare my *paan* for me in the afternoons. A village procurer sold her to me for three hundred rupees when she was only ten. Her parents had died of cholera. I gave her cod-liver oil every winter but she did not put on any weight. Then one day, the Inspector Saheb told me that I should stop trying to make her fat. 'She has the lithe body of a dancer,' he told me. Teach her to dance. She will charm your rich clients. I was planning to send her to a school to teach her some Bharatanatyam. But

God has taken away my sweet child. Sindhuthai, please don't tell anyone what really happened. The doctor saheb wrote in the certificate that her appendix burst."

"What is this appendix you are talking about? Is it the womb?" asked the old hag. "No, no, it is something else," said Ayee.

"Be more careful in the future, Lachmi," said Sindhuthai, "don't take chances. Rukmani should not be left to her fate. She too can become pregnant. She is well-developed." "Ah, Rukmani, she is not going to be in trouble," said Ayee. "The Inspector Sabeb has taken a great fancy to her. She is to be his keep. He is too old to have children. He must be quite old."

"No man is too old to procreate, Lachmi bai," said Sindhuthai. "I have known of a case when an eighty-year-old man married a twenty-year-old girl and gave her two sons. The Inspector Saheb is a lion among men. He is virile enough to populate one whole planet."

Ayee laughed and together with her laugh rose the dissonant cackle of the old hag.

"Do you want bangles?" asked a bangle seller who stopped at their front door. He held strapped to his shoulders a heavy case of wood and glass which contained bangles of myriad hues. Rukmani rushed forward to look at them. He sat down on the floor and took out a few cardboard rolls.

Each such roll bore on it about three dozens of plastic bangles. "May I have a look at the orange ones?" asked Saraswati, thrusting forward her dimpled arm. "Are they nylon ones?" she asked the bangle seller. "Yes they are expensive," he said. "Do you think I cannot afford your nylon bangles, my good man?" asked the dark girl with mocking eyes. The man gave her a knowing smile. "You can afford even gold ones, lady," he whispered. She laughed, and her laugh was like the tinkle of silver bells.

"Don't you want to buy some bangles for yourself, Rukmani?" asked Ayee. "The red ones of nylon will look good on your arms."

Rukmani shook her head. The bangles suddenly reminded her of Sita and then the desire to wear them on her own wrists went away. "No Ayee, I do not want any," she said.

Saraswati coaxed the man to put around her wrists, squeezing her palms, a dozen of the orange-coloured bangles. "What if I don't pay you?" she asked coequettishly. The man grinned sheepishly.

"You do not have to pay me," he said. "What kind of a businessman are you?" asked Saraswati taunting him. He smiled at her, noting for the first time her full breasts straining at the thin red voile of her choli and her wide haunches. "I am not much of a businessman," he retorted, "but I am a man all right. Do you want me to prove it to you?" Saraswati laughed aloud. She went inside the house to bring out the money. "Where are you from?" asked Ayee. "I am from Varanasi," said the man. "My brother has a *paan*-shop near Dadar and we stay together at Koliwada." "Are you making a lot of money selling *paan*," asked Ayee. "No, Mother. We are just pulling on..." Just then the Inspector Saheb entered the house. He was perspiring profusely. "Everything is taken care of," he said. "I want now to lie down and relax for an hour. Where is Rukmani? Ah here she is..."

Ayee thrust the little girl into the room with the Inspector Saheb. Rukmani leaned against the shut door and stared at the fat man on the bed. He had already taken off most of his clothes. His baton lay near the pillow. "Come to me, my moppet," he pleaded, his voice thickening with lust. Rukmani did not move.

"Are you angry with me, darling?" asked the man." Are you angry because I did not get you the foreign doll from

Churchgate today? You know how busy I was today with that girl's death and her cremation and all the technicalities connected with the events? Give me time. In three days' time the doll will be yours. You can call her Sita in honour of your playmate..."

Then Rukmani for the first time after her friend's death, broke down. She rushed towards the man and hid her sobbing face in the bushy growth of hair on his deep chest. "Papa, papa," she called out, sobbing, while the man, stupefied beyond words, kept stroking her curly hair. "Oh papa, take me away from here," she said, "Otherwise I too will die..."

The man kissed her forehead. Lust had suddenly retreated. "Papa. Is that what you called your father?" he asked.

"Yes," said Rukmani. "Papa was very fond of me. But he quarelled with my mother, and left our home without even telling me that he was going away. He did not ever return. Before Diwali, I used to wait for him near our house, hoping that he would bring me a new frock, but he did not come. He will never come to see me again, will he? He has forgotten me, hasn't he?"

"Don't cry, my child," said the Inspector, "you have me as your papa. I shall from now on treat you like my daughter. Is that enough, Rukmani?"

Rukmani lay cradled in his arms and fell asleep. She dreamt that Sita and she were travelling by a double-decker bus and that they were plucking ripe guavas from tall trees and eating them, seeds and all...

VI

When Mirathai returned, her clothes dishevelled and herself very hysterical, Ayee was taking a short nap in the afternoon, open-mouthed like a crocodile lying in wait for the dragonflies that might settle on its tongue. She looked hideous in sleep. Rukmani was seated on the floor watching Ayee asleep.

Mirathai fell on the ample bosom of the old woman and began to weep. "Help me Ayee," she cried, "the Inspector Saheb has ordered his constables to thrash him to death. They are torturing him at the police *chowki*. At this rate, he will fall down dead in an hour's time and I shall be a widow. Please go and tell them to stop beating him." Ayee stared at the young woman. No emotion showed on her dark face. "What has happened, Mira?" she asked slowly. "You have decided to return..."

"They are thrashing him to death," cried Mira. "Get up, Ayee, and tell the Inspector Saheb that he in not at fault. I was not kidnapped from here. I coaxed him to take me away. Then why should he bear the punishment while I am let off free?" "Where is this boy, Mira?" asked Ayee.

"He is at the police station," said Mirathai. "Please let him go free. I shall remain here for the rest of life."

Ayee got up from her charpoy and ate a *paan*. "All right, I shall go there and speak to the Inspector Saheb. You go inside and take a bath. Ask Radha to give you a good meal. You look as if you have been starving for a week." Mirathai kissed Ayee's hands in gratitude and went into the interior of the house. So our Mira has come back, said Ayee to herself. She walked towards the police station, escorted by Rukmani. "Falling in love with men is a dangerous thing," she told the little girl. "It is like tying oneself with a rope. If you do not love any man you remain free. Please remember that."

The young man had been beaten black and blue by the time Ayee reached the police station to plead with the Inspector, for mercy. But soon, she was carrying him back to her house in a tonga, triumphantly, while he sat with his face bent and tears streaming from his eyes. "It is not my fault," he mumbled once. But Ayee did not bother to converse with him.

When the tonga stopped near their house, Ayee asked the young man to alight. He was helped down by Rukmani. "All my bones are broken," said the boy.

"There is a letter for you today, mother of the house," exclaimed the postman stopping his cycle. "Open it and read it out to me, Rukmani," cried Ayee. "Can it be that my son has finally forgiven his sinner of a mother?"

The groaning young man limped into the house and sat down. The postman was lingering on to hear the contents of the long-awaited missive. Rukmani read: "Dear Ayee, I have remained silent for ten years but today my master who is a learned man showed me what true love means. He scolded me for having hurt you and for having abandoned you for years. He said that every profession has its own code of honour and that I ought not to have felt ashamed of you. He is a rich man owning a motor garage but he says that he will gladly give all his possessions if he were to be given back his mother who has been dead for ten years. You can earn money, you can get wives and children, but a mother lost is a mother lost forever, he said. Therefore, at his persuasion, I am writing to inform you that I shall be coming over to visit you this Saturday in the afternoon. Your loving son, Sadashiv Mane."

Ayee burst into tears. Rukmani felt tears filling her own eyes. Even the postman was turning emotional. "This is happy news," he said. Ayee took out of her waistband a rupee note and handed it to the postman. "See, how wise he has become, my son, my little son Sadashiv," said Ayee blowing her nose violently. Just then, Mira came out and saw the young man seated, still as a statue, on the floor. "Forgive me," she said, falling on the floor and clutching at his feet. "If I had not forced you to take me away from here nobody would have beaten you. Are you hurt badly? May I bring you some warm milk? Come and lie down for an hour."

"Mira, let him be," said Ayee. "Give him some peace. He has suffered all this because of you. Now leave him alone to find his own peace."

"What peace can he find without me?" asked Mira. "Is he not in love with me?"

The boy stretched himself on the floor and closed his eyes.

"Don't you love me still?" asked Mira.

"I don't know," said the boy.

"You go home to your mother now," said Ayee. "She must be so upset about your absence from home."

"She could not have been upset," said the young man, "because both she and my father were away visiting a relative at Poona. Today she is expected back at seven in the evening. I shall get home before she comes..."

"Was this to be merely a week's holiday, a short idyll?" asked Mira, a sob rising in her throat. "Were you lying to me when you said that we were going to live as husband and wife?"

The boy was silent.

"How old are you, son?" asked Ayee, chewing betel leaves. "I am nineteen," said the boy. "Go home to your mother and forget all about Mira," said Ayee. "Come to us after you get yourself a job and can afford to visit prostitutes."

Milira linched at the words. The boy rose, and folding his hands in a salute, he walked away.

"The ungrateful swine," hissed Mira. "He told me that he was twenty-four and that he had found a job at a mill. A liar. A stinking liar."

Mira threw out Saraswati's things from her former room. There was a lot of trouble then. Saraswati scratched Mira's fair face. "You slut," she called out to Mira, "you think you own this place? You run wild with a schoolboy for a week and return home as though nothing has happened. I shall not let you have this room. It belongs rightfully to me."

It was a question of seniority. Ayee could not take Mira's side this time. Mira had erred. Of that, there was no doubt at all. Saraswati was the most qualified of the lot, the one who was totally devoid of emotion and was the most professional of all. She deserved the best room.

Mira gave in and took a corner of the common hall where the juniors slept. She had to start rehabilitating herself again.

When the Inspector Saheb came, Ayee brought forth for him a plate of ladoos. He smiled at her. "What are you celebrating today?" he asked her. Then the letter was once again read out and once again tears flowed copiously from several pairs of eyes. "Your luck is changing, Lachmi bai," he said. Then he called Rukmani gesturing with hand and held out the large parcel which was with him. "Open it and see what I have brought for you, my daughter," he said.

Of course, it was the foreign doll. It did resemble Sita to some extent. Its vinyl-skin was very pale and its tummy had a bulge. Rukmani pressed it and made it squeak out the word Mummy. Rukmani kissed the doll all over its face and on its half-opened hands. "No kiss for your papa," asked the Inspector. She embraced him with her free hand and rubbed her nose on his shirt-front. "You are getting very sentimental," said Ayee to the Inspector. He nodded and gave another of his wide smiles. "Lachmi bai, I am an old man now," he said. "This child reminds me of my grand-daughter who is staying with her parents at Nagpur. She is sweet and affectionate like this one. Sends me a sweet letter every year at Diwali time."

"There is nothing like affection, Inspector Saheb," said Ayee. She kneaded the tobacco shreds with lime in the hollow of her left palm. "I am also not as young as I used to be. I wonder why I cannot leave this house in Saraswati's hands and go to Benares to die. I have enough money saved up to live in comfort until the last day of my life. Perhaps I shall carry someone with me, an old woman for company, perhaps our Sindhuthai. She has no relatives. I shall make up my mind after seeing my son this Saturday."

"We will miss you, Lachmi bai," said the Inspector. "This house will not be the same without you. And, Rukmani. Where will she go? She will have to be at the mercy of the new Ayee of the house..."

"I shall marry her off to my son," said Ayee. "Surely, he can now support a wife."

"Am I too early?" asked a client walking in, furtively glancing around. "You can never be too early in this house," said Saraswati coming forward to lead him into the room inside. He eyed her with appreciation.

"Would you like to spend some time with our Mira?" asked Ayee to Inspector. "You have always liked her."

"No, Lachmi bai, I do not feel like playing with a woman today," said the man, applying lime on the leaves of the betel carefully. "Something has died in me today."

"Perhaps something has been born inside you today," said Ayee with a tender grin. Rukmani's doll kept crying out Mummy, Mummy, Mummy...

18
WALLS

When he was leaving for the Bank he turned round and said, "I shall be late this evening. There is to be a shareholders' meeting today."

Sheer habit had compelled him to speak. No one listened to him anyway. Everybody was too busy to bother about his arrivals and departures. From the back seat of his car he surveyed the scene. His wife was trimming the grandchild's nails. His daughter seemed to be scolding the gardener. She was gesticulating wildly. The daughter-in-law turned the pages of a glossy magazine—idly and listlessly. The youngest son watched a cricket match on the television.

The car crunched the gravel of the pathway and paused for a minute at the gate where the dome-lanterns glowed faintly. They had forgotten to switch off the lights, as usual. "I told you yesterday that the rose-bush needs trimming...."

"And here is Kapil..."

He leaned back, exhausted at the discovery that he no longer loved his family. Quite often in recent times he had felt, while near all of them, that he was the lone intruder.

The greying woman would ask him, "Do you find the curds too sour?"

It was not possible to let her know that such things no longer mattered. He would continue eating in silence while all of them would converse, shout or argue. The thin girl with her painted fingernails would pick morsels of rice gingerly as if they were pearls. The young man would argue with his mother. He would sit among them steeped in loneliness. He was like a Ravi Varma model propped against Picasso's 'Guernica.' There was disharmony.

Like a parrot, the wife would repeat her opening gambit, "Do you find the curds too sour?"

Why did he remain silent at meal-time? After all he was with his own family. A family he had shaped to suit his taste. He had asked for sophistication, and he had got it. And yet the pride had faded with the years.

Perhaps there was no pride left. But after all each of them belonged to him. The middle-aged woman sporting pastel silks and diamond jewellery was his wife, this city-slick woman who spoke in several languages, conversing with her own grandchildren. Had she not changed within as imperceptibly as she had changed in her appearance over the years? Was she the Madhavi he had carried away from her village-home, her shyness as glittering as her wedding silks? He would not be able to answer such questions, for had he not forgotten those days, the brief season when the two of them dared to bare their ambitions, their desires? And, when the child had been born she had asked him,

"Shall we name him Bhaskaran, after my father?"

"Oh no, I shall not want him to be saddled with an old-fashioned name. I shall call him Manohar."

She had nodded in assent. That was twenty-eight years ago.

She would ask her daughter-in-law, "Lily, why hasn't Manohar returned home? It is half-past eight already."

"I do not know."

"Did he tell you that he would be late?"

"He doesn't tell me a thing."

After having been promoted as Sales Manager, Manohar made it a habit to return late. At the beginning of the year there was retrenchment in Manohar's office because of the fluctuations in the auto market.

What with the gratuity and benefits that had to be paid the survivors found themselves accepting smaller salaries. Manohar often remarked that labour was being pampered in India. Perhaps he was right. But when a youngster of Manohar's age made such a statement he was unnerved. Was Manohar a reactionary? The old capitalists were a vanishing tribe. They would be forgotten. But will Manohar be forgiven?

The car stopped. Only then did he realise that it was raining. A peon waited for him with an open umbrella. With a faint thrill he entered once again the portals of the institution he had worked in for thirty years. The hall was empty except for the clerk Pillay who sat stooped over his desk writing. Once he and Pillay had worked side by side as colleagues. In those days he called Pillay "Pillay Chettan". Gradually he had moved from the hall to the inner cabins. It was perhaps luck that made him the General Manager. When he began to pay eleven annas out of a rupee as income tax Pillay carried home his original pay packet. Looking at the bald head and the much laundered khadi shirt he asked himself why he had not done anything for Pillay. Pillay's performance was third rate. Like a circus dog leaping through a loop, Pillay went through the same movements day after day. Should he help Pillay only because he used to call him "Pillay Chettan" three decades ago?

He entered his room and removed his coat. The day's newspapers were already stacked on his table. Important financial news were underlined in red. The handiwork of Ramachandran, the new Assistant Manager. He was promoted recently. A wonder, considering his age. He was barely thirty-five. His capacity for hard work, the ability to smile away the slights and humiliations of common office-routine and his knack for observing decorum at all times, had definitely aided him in his climb upward. He spelt a secure future for the Bank. And yet, when the soft-spoken young man entered the room and moved about noiselessly, he began to feel uncomfortable.

The rain lashed at the glass-panes. He felt a perverse joy in opening the windows to let the rain wet the tiles. He remembered the thatched house in Palghat where the rain leaked into brass vessels all laid out to catch the water. Rain plopped against the metal with a twang.

"Narayanan Kutty, don't play with water. Finish your homework," his mother's voice. His mother, lean and tired looking into his eyes. His mother smiling at him....

Ramachandran pushed open the door and entered with a cough.

"Excuse me, Sir, I have a couple of important issues to discuss with you." Then catching sight of the open windows he rushed to close them, cursing the peon.

"It is my fault. I opened it."

Ramachandran spoke of the shareholders' meeting scheduled for the evening. The steel company that had asked for a loan was on the verge of a collapse. A partner had gone underground. He had made discreet enquiries to ascertain the facts. It would not be wise to lend them money....

"I shall remember it."

Ramachandran then read out the names of those who were to be promoted by the year-end. He wanted to know whether any name had been overlooked.

Pillay's name did not figure on Ramachandran's list.

"Include Pillay."

"What? That fossil? He is no good. In fact, I was planning to ask him to resign."

"I want Pillay to be promoted this year."

"Yes, Sir."

As Ramachandran went out looking flustered he re-entered the lonely world of reminiscences.

Am I preparing a balance sheet of my spent years, he asked himself. Of late he had been trying to draw happiness from memories. Sorrows, instead of fading out, began to haunt him. Man stands alone and rotates alone on his own axis. Loneliness is an appendage man cannot get rid of.

That night, before falling asleep, he said, "Madhavi, I want to resign from my job." She did not seem upset.

"Why?"

"I want to return to my village home. After all we two are no longer young."

She smiled. A gust of wind clamped the window shut. Outside a heavy downpour was in the offing.

19
GRANDFATHER

Grandfather sat up on his bed and said: "Thankam, when you leave here, you must take me with you."

Grandfather had cataract, but from under the opaque film, tears rolled down his cheeks.

"Father, please be reasonable," Thankam cried wringing her hands. "Frankly, I don't know what to do."

"Thankam, don't upset yourself listening to Father! You will be in real trouble if you do what he says," said the sister-in-law, chuckling cynically.

Thankam sat down on his bed and held his hand.

"We will come here after six months," she said. "The children's vacation will begin in May."

"You must take me with you," said the old man.

"Why do you want to leave this lovely house? Our flat in the city is very tiny. You are lucky to be living here, with trees all around you," said Thankam.

"I want to go away from here," he said. The white film over his eyes made Thankam uneasy.

"Thankam, don't upset yourself listening to him," said the sister-in-law. "You know what his age is. You know how difficult it is to manage him. He is totally dependent on others. You hardly have time to look after your children. Then why take on one more burden?"

Sister-in-law picked up an empty tumbler from the table and disappeared into the kitchen.

"You must take me with you," said the old man.

Thankam stroked the thin arm and said, "I don't know what I should do."

"Have you stopped needing me, Thankam?" asked Grandfather in his fractured voice. "Doesn't anyone want old people? Have I become unwanted?"

"What are you talking about?" Thankam asked, slightly irritated. "I don't mind taking you with me, but sister-in-law should not mind...."

"You must take me with you," repeated the old one.

"So you are planning to come with us to Bombay," said Thankam's husband, walking towards the bed.

"Father wants to come to Bombay," said Thankam.

"Father doesn't mean what he says. He was merely joking. You took him seriously," said her husband.

"Won't you take me to Bombay?" asked the father. "Won't you allow me to die in your own home, Thankam?"

"Please don't speak of death," said Thankam. "It is not time for you to think of dying."

"How old do you think I am?" asked the old man. "I shall be eighty-two this September. I should have been dead a long time ago. But I was lucky enough to see your children grow."

He wiped the tears from his face and folded his legs.

"Appu, there was a time when I cracked jokes," he said, turning to his son-in-law. "The time is over now. Now is the time to speak out from the mind. I hope you know what I mean."

"Maybe. But this time we shall not be able to take you with us. When we return from here in June we shall take you with us. This time we have not bought a ticket for you," said the son-in-law.

"I have told Thankam to take me with her. I have told her of my desire to live with her. Now it is up to her to decide what to do," said the old man, getting out of bed and moving towards the porch. Thankam hid her face with trembling hands and sobbed.

"What kind of madness is this?" shouted the husband, staring at her, "If you take him to Bombay at his age you will have to face the consequence of your action."

"But he is my father," said Thankam.

"Did I not have a father too?" asked the angry husband.

"The taxi has arrived," said the servant, looking in.

"All right. Carry our bags now," said the man.

After bidding everyone farewell Thankam turned towards her father. He was seated on the ledge of the patio, still as a statue.

"I shall come back in May," she said.

Grandfather did not utter a word. In the dimming light of the evening his right eye gleamed like a defective pearl. When the car had reached the corner Thankam turned round to look once more at her father. But by then darkness had fallen on him like a funerary shroud....

GLOSSARY

Amma	Mother
Ananda	Bliss
Behnji	Sister
Bhooth	Ghost
Chachaji	Uncle
Hafta	Week
Jhompdi	Hut
Lassi	Buttermilk
Mehndi	Henna
Mohalla	Locality
Moongphali	Groundnuts
Paan	Betel-leaf
Pithaji	Father
Pugree	Extortion of money by landlord from tenant
Pujari	Priest
Shingada	Water-chestnut
Sigri	Coal stove
Vaid	Physician